THE GREAT GREENE HEIST

VARIAN JOHNSON

SCHOLASTIC INC.

Copyright © 2014 by Varian Johnson

Arthur A. Levine Books hardcover edition designed by Nina Goffi, published by Arthur A. Levine Books, an imprint of Scholastic Inc., June 2014.

All rights reserved. Published by Scholastic Inc., *Publishers since 1920*. SCHOLASTIC, the LANTERN LOGO, and associated logos are trademarks and/or registered trademarks of Scholastic Inc.

ISBN 978-0-545-52553-4

15 14 13   19 20/0

Printed in the U.S.A.   40
This edition first printing 2015

Book design by Nina Goffi

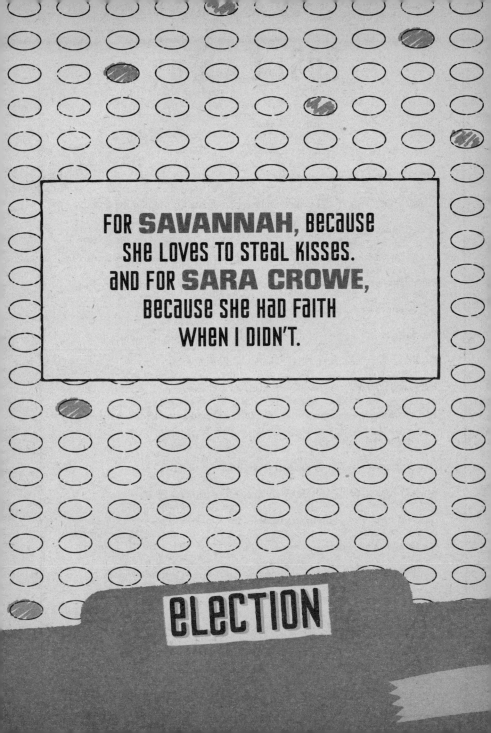

FOR **SAVANNAH**, BECAUSE
SHE LOVES TO STEAL KISSES.
AND FOR **SARA CROWE**,
BECAUSE SHE HAD FAITH
WHEN I DIDN'T.

ELECTION

CaST LIST

JACKSON GREENE — con artist (reformed)

CHARLIE DE LA CRUZ — editor of the *Maplewood Herald*

STEWART HOGAN — football player

GABRIELA DE LA CRUZ — basketball player; candidate for Maplewood Student
    Council President

LYNNE THURBER — basketball player; member of Gaby's campaign committee

KEITH SINCLAIR — basketball player; candidate for Maplewood Student
    Council President

WILTON JONES — member of the Gamer Club; Keith's right-hand man

DR. KELSEY — principal of Maplewood Middle School

HASHEMI LARIJANI — member of the Tech Club; inventor

SAMUEL GREENE — Jackson's older brother; freshman at the University
    of Pennsylvania

LINCOLN MILLER — chair of the Maplewood Honor Board

BRADLEY BOARDMAN — Art Geek; guidance office helper

CAROLINE APPLETON — administrative assistant

ALICIA GOLDMAN — administrative assistant

RAY BASILONE — locksmith at Basilone's Lock and Key; Samuel's friend

VICTOR CHO — Chess Team member

OMAR TURNER — basketball player (barely, according to Jackson)

CARMEN CLEAVER — member of the Environmental Action Team

MEGAN FELDMAN — president of the Tech Club; cheerleader

a NEW LeaF

As Jackson Greene sped past the Maplewood Middle School cafeteria — his trademark red tie skewed slightly to the left, a yellow No. 2 pencil balanced behind his ear, and a small spiral-bound notebook tucked in his right jacket pocket — he found himself dangerously close to sliding back into the warm confines of scheming and pranking.

Ignoring his empty stomach, he wove through the mob of students at the vending machines and continued toward the exit. Maybe he could convince Mrs. Kau to let him raid the machines during study hall next period. He could even offer to share his food with her — surely she had skipped the cafeteria's chicken enchiladas too.

Or maybe he could just forge a pass from the main office. Slip out of class. Pick the lock and sneak into the teachers' lounge. He knew all about the Hershey's bars Coach Rainey hid behind the stacks of dust-coated Styrofoam cups. The extra ham and swiss sandwich Mr. James, the security guard, always packed for a light afternoon snack. The box of mocha-caramel cupcakes Assistant Principal Nelson brought for the Junior National Honor Society's "Welcome Back" social.

It would have been easy. So easy.

Jackson pushed these thoughts out of his head. It was only September. He refused to jeopardize four months of model behavior for a quick snack, no matter how hungry he was. No matter how simple it would be.

No matter how much the idea tingled his spine.

He paused at the door and glanced at the GABY DE LA CRUZ FOR PRESIDENT poster, her name in big, bold, loopy letters. His fingers tightened around the note in his pocket.

When he reached the garden, he moved the note to his shirt pocket, then peeled off his blazer and folded it across the wooden fence. He was probably the only student at Maplewood — if not in all of Columbus, Ohio — who received notes the old-fashioned way. Most students used their cell phones to send messages, but he wasn't allowed to carry one during the school day. Yet another consequence of the Kelsey Job.

He pulled a pair of shears from the toolshed, then walked past red rose bushes and maroon marigolds to the far corner of the garden. He was almost finished pruning one of the peony bushes when he heard footsteps.

His long brown fingers tightened around the shears. "You're late," he said.

Charlie de la Cruz raised his hand to block the sun from his eyes. "Got stuck in the newsroom."

Of all the places they could meet, Charlie couldn't believe that Jackson wanted to talk out here. Sure, he knew that Jackson liked the Botany Club — probably as much as Charlie enjoyed being editor of the *Maplewood Herald* — but it was noon, and there wasn't a cloud in the sky. Charlie had only been outside for a few minutes, but his eyes were already beginning to burn, and he could feel the perspiration spreading across his forehead.

Of course, Jackson hadn't broken a sweat.

"Any day now," Jackson said, snipping another leaf. "You're the one who said Gaby needed help."

"She does." Charlie sneezed. "Stewart Hogan dropped out of the election. Keith's running for president."

Jackson missed the brown leaf he was aiming for and snipped a healthy green one instead. "Are you sure?"

"I just interviewed Naomi. She told me." Naomi Sinclair was running for Student Council secretary. She was also Keith Sinclair's cousin. If anyone would know, she would.

"Didn't the deadline to turn in applications already pass?" Jackson asked.

"According to my sources, there's some loophole that allows the school to extend the deadline in special circumstances."

"That's crazy. Mr. Pritchard would never —"

"Wasn't his call. From what I hear, Dr. Kelsey over-ruled him."

Jackson looked at Charlie. "Does Gaby know?"

"I don't think so. But word's beginning to spread. She'll find out soon enough." He paused to stifle another sneeze. "So what's the plan?" he asked, wiping his nose. "What should we do?"

"Nothing." Jackson cut another healthy leaf, barely missing his tie. "Gaby can still win."

"I don't know, Jackson. I don't trust Keith." Charlie stepped around the peony into the narrow space between flowerbeds. As he knelt beside Jackson, his stomach grumbled.

"There's a whole cafeteria full of food back in the building, you know."

"Do I look like I have a death wish?" Charlie asked.

Jackson finally smiled. "What did Naomi say? Did she give you any reason to believe that Keith was up to something?"

"She didn't tell me anything concrete. It's just a hunch." He elbowed Jackson. "You're the idea guy. If you were Keith, how would you guarantee your win?"

"I'd make signs and encourage students to vote."

"Come on. This is Keith Sinclair we're talking about. The guy you beat in the Blitz at the Fitz. The guy who squealed about the Mid-Day PDA —"

"Can't you call it the Kelsey Job?"

"You're the only one who calls it that." Charlie sneezed again. "And can we talk somewhere else? My allergies are killing me here."

"It's probably the cedar trees surrounding the football field that are making you sneeze." Jackson rose from his crouch, then helped Charlie to his feet. "And I don't plan cons anymore. Period." He squeezed past Charlie and walked to the toolshed.

Charlie's stomach grumbled again as he followed Jackson. "You can't stand by and do nothing."

Jackson returned the shears to the shed. "That's exactly what I plan to do."

"But —"

"I'm done talking about this." He turned around and waved a gray vinyl wallet at Charlie. "Look what I found."

"Hey!" Charlie felt his now-empty back pocket. "At least you can still make a decent pull."

"There's only one person I know who can do it better." Jackson opened the wallet, then turned it upside down. It was empty.

Charlie shrugged. "Information doesn't come cheap, you know."

Jackson pulled a few bills from his pocket and stuffed them into the wallet. "Get yourself some lunch. I'm sure you can find something in the vending machines." He tossed the wallet to Charlie, grabbed his jacket, then turned toward the building.

"Wait! What about Gaby?"

"You know your sister better than anyone." Jackson loosened his tie, pulling it even more to the left. "The last thing she wants is help from me."

JaCKSON'S EX-FRIEND

While Charlie stood in the garden and watched Jackson Greene walk away, his twin sister, Gabriela, sat in the cafeteria, jotting down some points she wanted to cover in her election campaign. However, her campaign committee, the Fighting Dolphins basketball team, was more interested in other matters.

Like boys and clothes and the next volleyball game and, well . . . boys.

"Guys, please," Gaby said, slapping the notebook on the table. "You can't force me to run for president and not help. I need a plan."

Lynne Thurber arched her eyebrow. "Hold on. We didn't *force* you —"

"You nominated me without telling me," Gaby said, wagging her finger at Lynne. Then she swung toward Fiona, who was ripping open a packet of ketchup with her teeth. "And you collected signatures without telling me."

Fiona squeezed the ketchup onto her plate. "You could have said no."

"But you —"

"Let me see that," Lynne said, grabbing the notebook. *"More computers in classrooms? A better selection of organic cafeteria food? More participation in Spirit Week?"* She dropped the notebook. "See. This is exactly why you should run."

"But —"

"Save it," Lynne replied. Although she was six inches taller than Gaby and Fiona, she slouched just enough to mask the difference. "Anyway, I don't see what the big deal is about the election. You don't see Fiona worrying about a slogan."

Fiona dipped a kettle chip into the pool of ketchup. "Yeah, but nobody knows — or cares — what the Student Council historian does." She popped the chip into her mouth. "And I'm running unopposed."

"Gaby might as well be unopposed. The only reason Stewart's even running is because Mr. Siegel promised him extra credit."

Gaby shook her head, letting her ponytail sway across her shoulders. "That doesn't matter. I still need to put a platform together," she said. "'Rule Number One: No matter how simple a job looks, always plan before you act. A poorly constructed plan usually yields undesirable results.'"

Fiona frowned. "'Rule Number One'? What's that all about?"

Gaby closed her eyes. *Jackson Greene and his stupid Code of Conduct.* "It's nothing. *Nada.* Just something I picked up." She broke off a piece of her pimento cheese sandwich. "Anyway, I see my platform as an opportunity to inform the student body about some of the projects we plan to —"

"Gaby, I know I said I'd be your campaign manager, but I'm not spending my lunch period planning for an election that's four weeks away." Lynne nodded toward the far end of the room, where most of the boys' basketball team sat. "Omar called you yesterday, right?"

Gaby glanced at Omar Turner. "We texted for almost an hour. Unlike you guys, he was happy to talk about the election."

"He's also looking for a date for the formal," Lynne said.

"You want her to go with Omar Turner?" Fiona wrinkled her nose. "He's kind of boring. And he wears too much cologne."

"He's cute." Lynne brushed the bangs from her face. "Cute beats boring any day."

"He hasn't asked me yet," Gaby said. "And maybe I don't want a date. Can't we all go together, like last year?"

"Last year we were children," Lynne said. "We're older now. More sophisticated. We're practically women."

Gaby bit into her sandwich, hoping it would stifle her laugh.

"I'm glad you talked to him," Lynne continued. "Honestly, you don't know a good thing when it's sitting right in front of you. At least Omar's not a liar and a cheat."

"It's not like Gaby and Jackson were a couple," Fiona said. "How was he supposed to know that she liked him?"

"I can't believe you're taking up for Jackson Greene! It's not Gaby's job to tell a boy how she feels. According to my sister, boys are supposed to figure that stuff out on their own." Lynne finally sat up, towering over the other girls. "And really, Katie Accord? I know she's popular and all, and as gorgeous as a supermodel, and a really good dancer, and —"

"You're not helping," Gaby said.

"Sorry." Lynne cleared her throat. "Katie's . . . um . . . She's not *supermodel* gorgeous. She's . . . um . . . just plain old, *regular* model gorgeous."

Fiona finished her chips. "Gaby, all I'm saying is that maybe — *technically* — you shouldn't be so mad at Jackson."

Gaby chewed on the inside of her cheek. She had tried to be like Fiona, had tried to look at this logically. She and Jackson had been friends. Just friends. She had never been brave enough to tell him how she really felt. So yes, technically he didn't do anything wrong, and therefore she shouldn't have been so upset.

But they had been friends who flirted with each other when they were playing basketball and video games; friends who had held hands three times; friends who had even hinted at going to the formal together this year. Whether she technically had the right to be upset or not did not matter. Plain and simple, Gabriela de la Cruz *was* upset, because the way she saw it, if Jackson liked Katie, then he didn't like her.

Gaby reached for her notebook. "I should talk to Omar. Maybe he'll have some ideas for my —"

"Gaby!" Heather Ames said, running up to the table, her face bright red. Heather was the videographer for the

basketball team. She usually ate lunch with the girls —
except on enchilada day.

Gaby stood up. "What's wrong?"

Heather fanned her face. "Talked to . . . Naomi. Big
problem . . . with . . . election." She gulped. "Keith . . .
Sinclair . . . is running . . . for president!"

THE OTHER CANDIDATE

Wilton Jones stood in the middle of the atrium, massaging his fingers. He checked the clock. The Gamer Club meeting started in less than five minutes. The guys were trying out a new first-person shooter, and he wanted to make sure his hands were limber. But the longer he waited, the more he worried he would miss out on playing the game entirely. They'd started the school year with an influx of new members — all thanks to Keith Sinclair.

Naomi walked into the atrium and made a beeline toward Wilton. "I just passed Keith in the hallway," she said. "He's being swarmed by a bunch of sixth graders. He could probably win the election on their votes alone."

Wilton smiled at Naomi. Even though she and Keith shared the same brown skin and black, curly hair, Naomi's eyes were much softer than Keith's. Kinder, even. "I can't believe Keith convinced you to run for secretary," he said.

"You know how Uncle Roderick is. He talked my dad into making me run. Something about resumes and transcripts and good schools. Plus, Dad promised to increase my allowance if I won." She tugged on one of her hoop earrings. "Money in the bank, especially since I'm the only candidate."

"An allowance bump," Wilton mumbled. "I should have thought of that." He was running for treasurer. Although he wasn't unopposed, he felt pretty good about his chances against Lonnie White.

"Can you give Keith my share of the signatures?" she asked, pressing the papers into his hands. "My mom's already outside."

He nodded. It looked like he wasn't going to make it to Gamer Club meeting on time, anyway.

After a few minutes, Keith finally appeared from the math wing, surrounded by a few sixth graders with basketballs. "Must be hard, being so popular," Wilton said, after Keith dismissed the last of the boys.

"What can I say? I took us to the District Championship last year, and people love a winner." Keith glanced at the papers in Wilton's hands. "Are those the signatures?"

"I got twenty, and Naomi got fifteen." He handed Keith the papers, then checked the clock. "You'd better hurry. Your application packet is due to Mr. Pritchard like now."

Keith squinted as he studied the nomination forms. With the twenty signatures he had collected, he was well over the fifty-signature requirement. "I'm not worried about Mr. Pritchard's stupid deadlines. It's not like he can kick me out of the election." He cut his eyes toward the main office on the other side of the atrium. "I should pop in and see Kelsey. I owe him some paperwork as well."

"I guess that means you'll be missing Gamer Club meeting again," Wilton said.

"I already beat *Alien Rebels*. Dad brought home a copy a month ago." Keith began to scroll through his phone. "I've been thinking — maybe we should quit the club. Once we get elected to Student Council, we won't have time for it. And you can always come to my house to play. My TV is better than the one in the AV room anyway."

"I actually like Gamer Club," Wilton said. "I also liked Tech Club. . . ."

"You should thank me for saving you from those losers. Megan is cool and all, but she has no business being president of the Tech Club. They only elected her because she's pretty."

"She's actually really smart."

"She's a cheerleader."

Wilton crossed his arms. "Angie's a cheerleader."

Most students would be intimidated if the football team's starting center stared them down, but Keith was too busy with his phone to notice. "Well, your sister's different. Obviously." He finally slipped his phone into his pocket. "Anything else?"

Wilton looked around, then stepped closer to Keith. "Have you thought this campaign through?" he asked. "Gaby's going to be tough to beat. A lot of people like her, and ever since the Blitz at the Fitz —"

"Jackson rigged that game!" Keith paused and took a deep breath. "I'll win. It's guaranteed."

"How?"

"That's what I'm about to find out." He punched Wilton's shoulder. "Tell the guys I'm sorry for not making the meeting. I'll make it up to them."

Keith crossed the atrium and entered the main office. Ignoring the two administrative assistants, he walked behind the counter to Dr. Kelsey's door, peeked through the window, and knocked. Dr. Kelsey waved him in. "Keith. At least you knocked this time." The principal removed his glasses and placed them on top of the draft of the first edition of the *Maplewood Herald*. The headline on the front page read, "Chicken Enchiladas: The New Phantom Menace."

"I figured you'd want this," Keith said, as he pulled a pink sheet from his folder and handed it to Dr. Kelsey.

"So all I have to do is fill this out, and your father will transfer the funds to my account?"

"You mean the school's account?"

"Yes," Dr. Kelsey said, squirming in his chair. "Of course."

Keith grinned. "My dad will transfer the funds to whatever account you like . . . as soon as the election is over." He leaned against the desk and looked down at Dr. Kelsey. "Have you figured out how you plan to — how should I say it — secure my win?"

"Why don't you let me worry about that?" Dr. Kelsey placed the form on his desk and rose from his chair, hoping that a subtle shift in height would remind Keith who was really in charge. He may have had to kiss up to Roderick Sinclair for donations and the occasional "favor," but he refused to do it to Roderick's son as well. "If that's all . . ."

"One more thing. Have you read the Student Council bylaws lately? Dad had one of his lawyers go over them last year, when I was having all that trouble with the Tech Club." Keith pulled a booklet from his backpack. "What if I told you I had a way to make some permanent changes to a few clubs — without you or any of the teachers getting involved?" He tossed the bylaws to Dr. Kelsey. "I tabbed it for you. Take a look."

Dr. Kelsey read the highlighted passage, and then read it again. "Let me guess. The Botany Club?"

"And the Tech Club."

Dr. Kelsey handed the bylaws back to Keith, thinking he certainly was a Sinclair, all right. No mercy.

"So what do you think?" Keith asked. "You get your money, I get the election, and a couple of clubs bite the dust in the process."

"A couple?" Dr. Kelsey glanced at the school newspaper. "Why stop at two?"

MEMORIES and MEMORABILIA

When Hashemi Larijani wheeled his bike around his house, the last thing he expected to see was the metal door to his shed propped open.

Given that the shed housed all of his tech equipment and memorabilia, the open door would have been troubling in itself. However, the object keeping the door ajar was the MAPE, or Most Awesome Phone Ever — the cell phone he had built from scratch. It contained an Omnitask 3000 multicore processor, tri-band Wi-Fi technology, two GPS chips, a twenty-megapixel camera with zoom and flash, voice recognition software, Bluetooth, an accelerometer, a gyroscope, and a slide-out keyboard. Its battery could last for a week on a single charge, and it could theoretically jump-start his mother's minivan. Sure, it weighed a pound and was too big to hold in one hand, but it was still technological perfection.

And now someone was using it as a *doorstop*.

Hashemi parked his bike outside the shed, stepped inside, and picked up the phone, allowing the door to slowly close behind him. Everything looked untouched, from his piles of *Popular Science* magazines to the Kirk, Spock, and McCoy action figures lining one of his shelves. He crammed the phone into his pocket and picked up the closest weapon he could find — a replica of the Lirpa that Kirk and Spock had used in *Star Trek* episode 34, "Amok Time."

He cleared his throat. "Hello? Anyone here?"

"Back here," a familiar voice replied.

Hashemi rounded a workbench and found Jackson Greene at the back of the shed, kneeling in front of a wooden door propped against the wall. Everything about the door was old and rotten — everything except its shiny silver lock.

"Um . . . Hi?" Hashemi said.

"Sorry," Jackson said, as he shimmied a long, metal pick into the deadbolt keyhole. "I got tired of being at home by myself. I figured I'd hang out here, but since you weren't around . . ."

"You could have emailed me. You didn't have to break into the shed."

"I tried to text you using the MOPE —"

"MAPE!"

"— but it doesn't work."

Hashemi nodded. "It's a beta version. I had to delete the dialing commands to make room for the gyroscope software."

Jackson repositioned the pick and squinted at the lock. "Yeah. That makes perfect sense."

"So how did you break into my shed, if you don't mind me asking?"

Jackson glanced at the open padlock by his feet. "03-22-33. Captain Kirk's birthday, right?"

Hashemi scratched his head. "How did —"

"Seriously? You're carrying a *Star Trek* battle axe."

"It's called a Lirpa."

"All I'm saying is, your lock combination is way too easy to crack." Jackson removed the pick from the keyhole, grabbed a screwdriver, and began disassembling the deadbolt. "At least I got through one lock today."

"Still can't crack the Guttenbabel?"

Jackson shook his head as he wrapped the deadbolt in a thick shop rag and placed it by the base of the door. Pickable or not, the Guttenbabel 4200 was a thing of beauty, and he didn't want to scuff it up. "So what else happened today?" he asked.

"Nothing — except Megan bailed on us right after the Tech Club meeting." Hashemi brushed some loose green and red wires from a stool, then slumped onto the seat. "We were all supposed to hang out at Keno's house to work on the robot for Regionals, but she had other plans."

"She probably had to run off and share the latest gossip with the Drama Mafia."

"Jackson . . ."

"What's she doing helping you guys with the robot anyway? I thought she was a chemistry geek."

"Chemistry, electronics, programming — she can do it all. She's like the Thomas Edison of middle school. Except, you know, pretty. And not dead."

Jackson dusted off his jeans, which were still speckled

with bits of leaves, petals, and pollen. "So is that it? Nothing else crazy happened today?"

"Yeah. Why, what did I miss?"

"I'll tell you later. Let's play some *Ultimate Fantasy III*."

"No!" Hashemi leapt from his chair. "Anything but that!"

"Oh-kay." Jackson picked up the padlock and tossed it to Hashemi. "How about something to eat, then? My house or yours?"

Hashemi placed the lock on the table, then wiped his glasses. "What type of ice cream do you have?"

Jackson thought for a minute. "Vanilla."

"My place," Hashemi said. "I have chocolate chip."

After a quick pit stop in the kitchen, they headed to Hashemi's bedroom. It rivaled the size of most garages, yet it still overflowed with junk.

Or rather, memorabilia.

Hashemi took a bite of ice cream as Jackson flipped through his video game collection. "*Sk8tr Boiz Dance Explosion?*" Jackson asked. "Really? Do you have a set of Sk8tr Boiz dolls as well?"

"My doctor says it counts as exercise," Hashemi said.

Jackson tossed *Dance Explosion* to the side and settled on *Zombie Pirates*. Ten minutes later, they had restarted the game four times, as they both kept making careless mistakes.

"Clearly, this hasn't been a good day for either of us," Jackson said after he accidentally sliced off Hashemi's hand with a cutlass. He paused the game. "There's something I should tell —"

"She has a boyfriend."

"What?"

"Megan Feldman. She has a boyfriend. That's why she bailed on us." Hashemi stared into his half-full bowl of ice cream. "He has a copy of *Ultimate Fantasy IV.*"

"That's not supposed to come out until Christmas!"

"I know," Hashemi said. *"Ultimate Fantasy IV!* How am I supposed to compete with that?"

"Do you know who has it? Is it a student at Maplewood?" Thanks to his father's job, Keith often received new games before they were officially released. He had had an impressive collection until Jackson . . . *liberated* the games during Keith's birthday party last year.

"Don't worry. Megan promised us that it wasn't Keith." Hashemi scooped an extra-large chunk of ice cream. "I guess I thought, with the formal and all . . . If she were going and I were going, maybe I could ask . . ."

"You're better off. Who wants to go to a stupid dance anyway? Especially with Megan Feldman. She'd just blab about it to the entire school." Jackson looked out the window, toward the basketball hoop hanging above his garage next door.

"How many times does she have to apologize?" Hashemi asked. "She didn't know her friends were going to tell Keith —"

"Forget it," Jackson said. "It's done. I'm over it." He finished his ice cream and placed the bowl on the desk. "There's something important I need to tell you. Just promise you won't freak out."

"Wait. *You're* not Megan's boyfriend, are you?"

"Of course not." Jackson sighed. "Keith Sinclair is running for Student Council president."

Hashemi's entire body tensed. "Keith Sinclair? No! He'll ruin us! He'll make us quit the Tech Club and join his stupid Gamer Club!"

"You're overreacting," Jackson said.

"No, I'm not," Hashemi said. "He'll kill the club! He'll cut our funding to nothing!"

"The entire Student Council, including classroom representatives, votes on the budget."

Hashemi pushed his glasses up the bridge of his nose. "Not if they don't reach quorum. In those instances, the Executive Council can pass rules on Student Council's behalf. That includes budgets." He placed his bowl on top of a stack of technical journals. "That's exactly what happened last year."

"You mean when Keith convinced Student Council to give the Gamer Club part of the Tech Club's money?"

"That's how it ended up. But first Keith tried to get the Executive Council to move *all* the money over to the Gamer Club. He even showed them in the bylaws where they could do it. Lucky for us, Gaby made it to the meeting and stopped them. We still had to raise money for Nationals, but not as much as we would have if they had taken it all."

Jackson reached for his jacket, which he had laid across Hashemi's bed. Maplewood had some crazy rules when it came to the way student organizations were run — all designed to "empower students to make their own responsible choices" — but he had never heard of anyone actually using the Student Council bylaws to limit a club's funding. "How many classroom reps have to be in attendance to meet quorum?" he asked as he fumbled through the pockets for his notebook.

"Seventy-five percent, I think."

Jackson flipped open his notebook and did the math. "That's what — twenty students? Twenty-five? There's no way that many reps make it to every meeting." He turned to a blank page and began listing the candidates running for office. "So are you really telling me that the five kids on the Executive Council can decide the budget for every student organization?"

"Not even that many. They just need a majority vote."

Jackson stopped writing. He looked at Hashemi, but didn't know what to say.

Hashemi frowned. "What is it?"

"Wilton's running for treasurer, Naomi for secretary, and Keith for president." He tapped his pencil against his leg. "That's three out of five. . . . A majority vote."

Hashemi groaned. "We're dead!"

"Hash —"

"I'm telling you, Jackson. He did it before. He'll do it again. And he won't stop with the Tech Club."

"Don't worry. Gaby can beat him," Jackson said. "But you should let the Tech Club know what's going on. Gaby'll need all the support she can get."

Hashemi tugged at his collar. "Or maybe there's another way. . . ."

Jackson closed his notebook. "I have no idea what you're talking about."

"Come on, Jackson. You have a plan, right?" Hashemi clasped his hands together like he was praying for divine intervention. "Please tell me you have a plan."

Jackson turned toward the still-paused video game. "You know I don't do that stuff anymore."

"But you can't let Keith win! It was his fault you got caught during the Mid-Day PDA —"

"You're calling it that too?"

"And now he's going to beat your ex-friend, who happens to be a girl who wasn't your girlfriend but who *could* have been your girlfriend if you hadn't got caught kissing —"

"Land the plane, Hash."

"I'm just wondering . . . I know he's mad at the Tech Club, but he hates you one thousand times more. Do you think he's doing this — trying to beat Gaby — just to get back at you?"

Jackson shrugged. "Maybe. I don't know why, though. Gaby doesn't want anything to do with me."

"When's the last time you tried to talk to her?"

"Fourth of July."

"How did it go?"

"Other than the fact that she slammed the door in my face, it went great."

Hashemi rose from his chair.

"Where are you going?" Jackson asked.

"To get more ice cream," he said. "This is a two-bowl type of day."

UNREQUESTED ADVICE

"Sorry for the late meal," Jackson's father said as he slid into his chair beside Jackson's mother. "Crazy day at the office. Everyone dig in."

Donald Greene, in an attempt to pitch in more around the house, had offered to take over the cooking duties once a week. Inspired by his own upbringing, he chose to cook traditional Southern soul food dishes — except, at the request of his wife, with less fat and more vegetables. So as Jackson hacked away at his "traditional but healthy" meal of "extra-blackened" fried catfish, soggy sweet peas, and mushy brown rice, he wondered if he would be better off with the Maplewood chicken enchiladas.

"I told your mother this earlier — I have to jet to DC to debrief HQ on the Bellingham case next week. Just a quick day trip." As a special agent for the IRS Criminal Investigation Division, Donald Greene often traveled, especially when he was working on a major case. "Turns out Bellingham used a network of pizza delivery boys to launder his drug money."

"Donald, that sounds like that job your father pulled once, when he —"

"Allegedly," Jackson and his father said at the same time.

Miranda Greene rolled her eyes. "A job he *allegedly* pulled, when he was trying to get an animal handler to train a . . ." She turned to Jackson. "What am I thinking? You do *not* need to hear another story about your grandfather's life of crime."

Donald Greene picked up his knife and went to work on his food. "Don't worry. It's not like Jackson has access to chimpanzees." He paused. "Wait — when's the circus coming into town again?"

Jackson's mother speared a few peas, which deflated the instant she pierced them. "And as soon as your father gets back, I have to leave for a conference."

"What's your talk on this time?" his father asked.

She smiled. "'The Nuclear Magnetic Resonance Study of Water Diffusion in the Olfactory Nerve of Colorado River Cutthroat Trout.'"

Donald Greene winked as he nudged his son. "If Ohio State paid your mom by the syllable, we'd be rich." After waiting for but not receiving a reply from Jackson, he asked, "And how was your day?"

"Fine. Nothing really happened. Not to me, anyway." Jackson kept his face on his plate as he spoke.

"That's what I like to hear," Miranda Greene said. "A boring day is a good day."

Donald Greene coughed. "There's nothing wrong with a little excitement —"

"Jackson can be excited next year, once he's in high school."

His father took a drink of his home-brewed unsweetened iced tea, which looked more like muddy water. "I was looking at the school schedule this morning and noticed that the Fall Formal is coming up. Are you thinking about going? I've got a killer powder-blue suit you can borrow. Dad passed it down to me. Butterfly collar, ruffles — I'm telling you, it's a classic."

Jackson reached for his water. "Um, no, thanks."

"Suit yourself," his father said, then chuckled at his own little joke. "But still, you should go to the dance."

"Aren't I still on punishment?"

Miranda Greene folded her napkin and dabbed at the corner of her mouth. "Your father thinks —"

Donald Greene cleared his throat.

"Your father and I both think you should socialize more with your friends. It's been four months since that . . . unfortunate incident, and your behavior has been nothing but exemplary."

Jackson put his fork down. "I don't need to go to the formal to see my friends. I was just at Hash's today, and Charlie was over here last week."

Miranda Greene glanced at her husband. "We were thinking —"

"Not that we're trying to dictate your love life —"

"This is, of course, your decision —"

"You should ask Gaby to the dance."

Jackson felt his body slide a few inches lower in his chair.

"She's smart," his mother said. "She was just in the *Dispatch* last week for academic excellence. I used to have a copy around here. . . ."

Jackson slid another inch. The newspaper now resided at the bottom of his desk drawer.

"She plays basketball," his father said. "And she's a looker."

"Donald!"

His father shrugged. "Well, she is."

"Jackson, we're not trying to force you to date, nor are we trying to force you to date *her*," his mother said. "But it's clear she's got a good head on her shoulders. She might be a good influence on you."

Jackson studied his parents while he took another sip of water. His father's face was a blank slate — he seemed to be too busy shoveling food into his mouth to be bothered with any other thoughts. His mother, on the other hand, kept looking at his father, her fingers spinning her plain gold wedding band.

Donald Greene swallowed his food and said, "Stop trying to read us, Jackson. You don't think my dad taught me the same things he taught you and Samuel —"

"Does this have anything to do with the girl from Boston that Samuel's dating?" Jackson asked.

"You mean the girl not currently enrolled in school, because she's 'discovering herself'? The girl with the tiger lily tattooed on her neck?" Miranda Greene stabbed her catfish. "Of course this has nothing to do with her."

"She doesn't like basketball," his father grumbled. "What does Samuel see in a girl who doesn't even like basketball?"

Jackson pushed away from the table. "Thanks again, but I'll pass on the suit and the formal."

He began to pick up his plate, but his mother stopped him. "Leave it. I'm heading to the kitchen in a few minutes," she said. She placed her hand on his arm. "And honey, Gaby won't be mad at you forever."

"What makes you think me not wanting to go to the formal has anything to do with her?"

Jackson's father laughed. "You're not the only one that can read people, kiddo."

Miranda Greene sighed. "Don't get me wrong — I don't know what possessed you to kiss that other girl. Really, teenage boys are so dumb! But Gaby understands how sorry you are. She'll come around."

"And if things don't work out with Gaby, you could always ask that Katie Accord to the formal," his father said, leaning back in his chair. "I have to admit, that took some guts. Even Samuel wasn't bold enough to kiss the superintendent's daughter in public at Maplewood!"

"Donald, don't encourage him."

"I'm not —"

"I'll be in my room," Jackson said, although he suspected his parents were too busy arguing to hear him leave.

There was an email waiting for Jackson when he opened his laptop.

FROM: Lincoln.Miller@maplewoodmiddleschool.edu
TO: election.candidates@maplewoodmiddleschool.edu
BCC: Jackson.Greene@maplewoodmiddleschool.edu

I have fielded a few questions concerning the nominations for the upcoming Student Council elections. In order to ensure a transparent process, I'd like to meet with the candidates and any interested students to discuss the election. We will meet in the auditorium tomorrow at 7:30 a.m. Please come. . . . After all, this is YOUR election.

Lincoln Miller
Chair, Maplewood Student Honor Board

Jackson stared at the message for a few seconds, trying to will himself to press the DELETE key. Finally, he saved the message to a folder, grabbed his clock, and set the alarm for 6:30 a.m.

an INNOCENT BYSTaNDER

Gaby entered the auditorium and paused. She had forgotten to pick up her contacts from Walgreens last night, and her eyes always took a little longer to adjust to changes in brightness when she wore her glasses. Once she had her bearings, she made her way to the front row and sat down next to Fiona. Even though food wasn't allowed in the auditorium, Fiona was munching on a fruit bar and slurping down an iced coffee.

Omar Turner sat just across the aisle. When he saw her, he smiled and waved. After a second of hesitation, Gaby waved back. Omar wasn't running — he was too busy with basketball and MATHCOUNTS and Model UN to serve on Student Council — but he had offered to serve as Gaby's "strategic advisor" for the campaign.

Gaby's expression changed when she saw Keith. He had the nerve to smile at her, and then *wink*. She wanted to flash a hand sign that would show him just how much she didn't appreciate that wink, but that wasn't an action becoming of a Student Council officer.

Plus, Mr. Pritchard was standing right in front of her.

"Why didn't you wait for me this morning?" Charlie asked as he plopped into the seat beside her.

"I didn't know you were coming," she said. "I thought Amanda was covering this for the newspaper."

"I'm here because of you," he said. "Someone's got to have your back against Keith. I know I can't prove it, but he's up to something."

"We've already gone over this, Charlie. The last thing I want is you and Jackson using my campaign to wage a war against Keith Sinclair. I can handle him on my own."

Charlie snorted. "Well, you don't have to worry about Jackson. He's taking a pass. He's . . . retired."

Gaby tugged her ponytail. "Good. You should do the same."

A few minutes later, Lincoln Miller took the stage. He coughed into the microphone, and it screeched. "I'm glad you all could make it this morning, especially on such short notice. I was worried that no one would see the email." He glanced at Mr. Pritchard, who sat stone-faced on the edge of the stage. "I know there are some concerns about the nominations process," he said, "so Mr. Pritchard and I wanted to address any questions now, before we move on to the next step in the election." He tapped his note cards against the podium. "As most of you know, Stewart Hogan dropped out of the race on Friday afternoon. Dr. Kelsey felt that, in the spirit of presenting the student body with multiple options, we should allow Keith to enter even though the deadline had passed."

The auditorium buzzed.

"I know some of you are unhappy with this," Lincoln continued. "But the bylaws clearly state that the advisor or the administration can extend the deadline as necessary to encourage competition." He exhaled. "Any questions?"

Charlie looked around. Everyone was looking at their laps or the floor. Everyone except Keith. Charlie finally raised his hand.

"Carlito . . ." Gaby whispered. "Let it go."

"Don't worry," he mumbled back. Not waiting to be recognized, he said, "I don't have any issues with Keith running for president as long as his application packet was submitted correctly."

"It was," Keith piped up from his chair.

Charlie kept his gaze on Lincoln. "When did Keith turn in the forms again?"

Lincoln looked at Mr. Pritchard. "I'm not sure. . . ."

Mr. Pritchard rubbed his graying beard. "Keith turned in his packet this morning."

Charlie leaned forward. "But I thought it was due yesterday!"

"Keith was a little late turning in his paperwork, but Dr. Kelsey felt that we should accept it, given the circumstances," Mr. Pritchard said. "As Lincoln stated, this flexibility is well within the bylaws."

"I wonder what else the bylaws clearly state?" Charlie muttered.

It was meant to be a snide comment, but Mr. Pritchard decided to answer the question. "The bylaws also allow the administration to aid the Honor Board in the election process," he said. "Which means the main office will be responsible for collecting and tallying the votes."

"But . . . That's my job," Lincoln said.

"I know," Mr. Pritchard said, his voice quiet. "I'm sorry." He faced the audience. "Unless there are any other questions, I'll see you all after the election, at our first Student Council meeting next month."

As the other students exited the auditorium, Charlie dragged Gaby toward Mr. Pritchard. Lincoln was already in front of him. "But it's my job to oversee the election," Lincoln said. "It's always been the chairperson's job. It's in the bylaws."

"Dr. Kelsey doesn't want you wasting your time collecting and counting ballots."

"So who's going to do it?" Lincoln asked.

"I don't know." Mr. Pritchard placed his hand on Lincoln's bony shoulder. "I'll talk to Dr. Kelsey again. Maybe I can convince him to let you help with the scoring." He turned to Charlie and Gaby. "I'm sorry about all of this, Gabriela. I'm sure I'm not supposed to say this, but I was thrilled when I learned that you were running. I want you to know that I'm rooting for you."

Gaby nodded. "Thank you."

"There has to be something you can do," Charlie said. He looked at Keith, who stood by the door with a few of his friends. "It's not fair."

"I'm sorry," Mr. Pritchard said, for what seemed like the hundredth time. "My hands are tied."

Charlie and Gaby returned to their seats to pick up their bags. Keith walked over to them. "I just wanted to wish you good luck," he said to Gaby, extending his hand.

Gaby glanced at Keith's thin, wiry fingers. She almost expected him to be hiding a shocker in his palm. Finally, she shook his hand. "Good luck to you too."

"Do you mind if we talk for a few minutes? In private?" he asked. "No offense, but I don't usually waste my time with sidekicks." His eyes cut over to Charlie.

Charlie smiled. "Are you still mad about the Shakedown in Shimmering Hills? You lost those video games fair and square. But I'm sure the Tech Club really appreciated how you and Jackson donated them to their fund-raising drive."

Gaby shook her head. "Charlie . . ."

"Jackson stole those games," Keith said. "Cheated me out of them."

"Or maybe you're worried that Gaby will beat you as badly as she and Jackson did during the Blitz at the Fitz?" Charlie continued. "What was the score again? Twenty-one to seven? To ten? I didn't know two-on-two games could be so lopsided. . . ."

"Jackson bent the rim," Keith said.

"Not according to the ref."

"Then he paid off the officials."

"That sounds like a page from *your* handbook."

Keith crossed his arms. "At least I don't have to worry about Jackson cheating anymore. Ever since he got busted —"

"You mean ever since you squealed —"

"Enough!" Gaby nudged her brother. "Go on. I'll catch up with you later."

Charlie slung his book bag over his shoulder. "Don't talk to him for too long. You know rats carry germs," he said before leaving the auditorium.

Gaby placed her hands on her hips. "What do you want, Keith?"

He rubbed the back of his neck. "I just want you to know . . . me running for president . . . It's nothing personal."

"Um . . . Okay."

"I mean, while it would be nice if you would apologize for cheating during the Blitz at the — during that pickup game, I won't hold it against you. I'll even promise to reduce paper waste and add more organic food to the cafeteria menu after I win."

"That's my platform!"

"As my dad says, it doesn't matter who comes up with the initial idea. Success takes a group effort."

Gaby rolled her eyes. That was almost as cheesy as Jackson's Code of Conduct.

"Come on, Gaby. Think about it this way — I win the election, you save the environment. Everybody benefits." Keith's face turned serious. "I'm going to win, Gaby."

"Are we finished here? I have someplace I need to be."

He shrugged. "Don't say I didn't warn you."

As Keith walked to his seat to collect his books, Gaby glanced toward the rear of the auditorium. A shadowy figure had paused in the doorway. The lighting was low, but Gaby could just make out a red tie against a white shirt as the figure slipped through the exit.

TIME **WAITS** FOR NO **MAN**

Jackson paused at the entrance to the library and stared at the sign taped to the door. He told himself to breathe, that this would be a quick, easy chat. That she wouldn't mind what he was about to say. That the last four months didn't matter.

He slowly opened the door. Gaby sat at one of the large tables, her eyes glued to her paper, her hand scribbling away. He proceeded toward her, his feet silent against the red plush carpet. "Hey," he said, his voice soft and reserved. "Got a few minutes to talk?"

Gaby tensed as she dropped her pencil and covered her notebook paper with her hands. "What do you want?" she asked.

Jackson took a small step backward. "I know I said I wouldn't talk to you —"

"Then why are you starting now?"

"It'll only take five minutes."

"I have a meeting." She glanced at the wall clock across

the room. "My campaign committee will be here any second."

Jackson focused on Gaby's face. He liked how the rectangular frames of her glasses made her brown eyes look even darker. Wider. More mysterious.

"What happened to your contacts?" he asked. "Allergies? The pollen count is pretty high."

He suppressed a groan as soon as the words left his mouth. He hadn't had a real conversation with Gaby in four months, and all he could think to talk about was pollen?

"You know I'm not allergic to stuff like that." She fiddled with the glasses. "I forgot to get my contacts prescription filled."

"The glasses are nice. They make your eyes look . . ." He cleared his throat. "You should forget your contacts more often."

Gaby sighed, and her shoulders relaxed. "Five minutes, Jackson." She flipped over her sheet of paper.

"I'll make this quick," he said as he sat down across from her. "I'm here to volunteer for your campaign."

Gaby shook her head. "I don't think that's a good idea."

"You need someone on your team who understands how Keith thinks. He'll play dirty. He'll break the rules."

"And you know all about that, don't you?"

"I've stopped." Jackson glanced at the clock. "Mostly."

"I saw you leaving the auditorium," she said. "You're not as sneaky as you used to be."

"I'm rusty." He put his hands flat against the table and looked at Gaby's fingers, inches away from his. The last time they had held hands was in this library, at this very table. "What were you and Keith talking about?"

"He was just telling me how he'd steal my ideas if he won."

"Of course. He's not smart enough to come up with something like an organic food station on his own."

Gaby blinked. "You read my posters?"

He nodded, then looked down at the table. "I just want to help."

"Charlie thinks he's up to something," Gaby said. "You do too, don't you?"

Jackson remained still for a few seconds, then nodded again. "You can beat him." His voice cracked as he spoke.

"You really are getting rusty." Gaby tilted her head as she stared at Jackson. Finally, she flipped the sheet over and slid it toward him. "Got any ideas for my campaign plan? I'm still having trouble sorting out the details."

Jackson had barely begun reading when Omar Turner burst into the library. Omar was the starting center on the boys' basketball team, though that was due more to his size than his skills. He cut his eyes toward Jackson before turning back toward Gaby. "We were wondering what happened to you," he said. "We tried to call, but your cell phone is off."

"What do you mean?" Gaby asked. "We're supposed to be meeting in here."

Omar shook his head. "There's a note taped to the door saying that the meeting moved to the auditorium."

"What? But I didn't —" Gaby let out a huff of air and narrowed her eyes at Jackson. "A note, huh?"

Jackson stood, then reached into his right pocket and pulled out a black marker. "I found this outside the library door."

"So much for being retired," Gaby mumbled. "Omar, will you do me a favor and get the rest of the committee?"

"Some of the girls have already left. We've been waiting for almost ten minutes."

"But the meeting wasn't supposed to start until . . ." She glanced at the clock. "The second hand isn't moving, is it?"

Jackson smiled as he placed a shiny nine-volt battery beside the black marker. "I found this with the marker. Honest."

Omar stretched his face into a tight smile. "So are you on Gaby's campaign committee?" he asked Jackson. "I haven't seen you at the meetings."

Gaby jumped out of her seat, which made the plastic chair tumble backward. "No. Jackson's not . . . He won't —"

"I came to volunteer," Jackson said as he tried to stand taller.

"Thanks for the offer, but . . ." Gaby circled the table and gave Omar a sideways, two-second hug. "My campaign committee and I can take it from here."

Jackson finally stopped smiling.

"Omar, can you get the others?" she asked, her cheeks turning red. "We have a lot to go over today."

Omar nodded. "I'll . . . I'll get the others. Of course." He was so busy grinning, he ran into a bookshelf. Twice.

"I thought you said you didn't break the rules any-more," Gaby said once Omar was gone.

"I said *mostly*." Jackson held open his hands as if he were signaling defeat. "Some rules deserve to be broken for the greater good."

"The greater good?" she said. "You promised you were going to stop."

"I needed to talk to you."

"And you couldn't just come up to me like a normal person?"

"The last time I tried to talk to you 'like a normal person,' you slammed a door in my face."

"At least I said good-bye before I closed it."

"Slammed it."

"Closed it. With feeling."

He rubbed his nose. "I felt it, all right."

She shook her head, her ponytail swinging like a whip, and picked up the notebook paper from the table. "Mind tossing this in the recycle bin? Since you were just leaving and all?" She wadded up the paper and threw it at Jackson.

It was a perfect pass — right into his chest. Straight toward his heart.

a CHANGE OF HEART

The next morning, Jackson arrived at school with a sour taste in his mouth. As much as he wanted to blame it on his father's leftover fried catfish, he knew it was due to his conversation with Gaby.

Hashemi didn't look any better as he walked up to Jackson's locker. His hair was matted on one side of his head, and his clothes looked like he'd slept in them.

"I found out who has a copy of *Ultimate Fantasy IV*. Mr. All-American. Stewart Hogan. *That's* who Megan's been hanging out with." He shook his head. "Stupid jocks. And I thought nerds were supposed to be the cool guys."

"So that's how he got him to drop out!" Jackson slammed his locker shut. "I'll catch you later."

Jackson wove through the hallway toward Charlie's locker. He arrived just as Charlie was spinning his combination.

"Remember what I was telling you about Megan Feldman's mystery boyfriend and *Ultimate Fantasy IV*?"

Jackson asked, leaning against the row of battered metal lockers. "It's Stewart. *He* has *UF IV.*"

Charlie opened his locker and began to remove books from his book bag.

"Quite a coincidence, huh?" Jackson continued. "Stewart gets his hands on the hottest game around, right at the same time he drops out of the presidential race."

Charlie pulled what looked to be a smashed sandwich from the bottom of his bag.

"That means you were right." He nudged Charlie. "Keith *is* up to something."

Charlie sniffed the sandwich, then stuck it on the top of his Algebra book.

"Charlie?"

Charlie paused, his hand on the locker door.

"Okay," Jackson said. "I'm sorry."

"And . . ."

"I'm sorry and you were right."

"You're sorry and I was right and I'm a genius and you owe me ten dollars."

"Don't push it."

Charlie smiled. "I heard about Stewart last night. Figured Hashemi would fill you in today." He closed his locker. "Come to the library after school. There's someone I want you to meet."

That afternoon, Jackson sat down with Charlie at the same table he and Gaby had shared yesterday. A wiry boy took the seat across from them. Jackson assumed the boy was in sixth grade, but he looked no older than ten. Paint flecks spotted his polo, and his fingernails were caked with dried red clay.

"You're a member of the Art Geeks?" Jackson asked.

The boy's eyes widened. "How did you know that?"

"Lucky guess." Jackson reached across the table. "I'm Jackson —"

"I know exactly who you are," the boy said as he clamped onto Jackson's hand. "I heard all about how you hacked into the computer system last year and scheduled a four-hour lunch for everyone —"

"Allegedly," Jackson said.

"And how you stole the goat mascot from Riggins Middle School and sold it on eBay —"

"I can neither confirm nor deny that act."

"And then there was the Mid-Day PDA. Who else would have the guts to kiss a Mona Lisa like Keith Sinclair's girlfriend?"

"Ex-girlfriend," Jackson said, pulling his hand free from the boy's grip. "And it was just a peck."

"That's not what I heard."

Jackson loosened his tie. "You're in sixth grade, right? How did you even hear about that stuff?"

"Are you kidding? There are whole websites dedicated to the Infamous Jackson Greene."

The Infamous Jackson Greene. Jackson cut his eyes at Charlie. "Really?"

"Don't look at me," Charlie said. "Phoebe handles the web content for the *Herald.*"

Jackson leaned back in his chair. "Since you know so much about me, can you at least tell me your name?"

"Oh. I'm Bradley Boardman."

"Bradley's the fourth period guidance office helper. He also helps out in the main office." Charlie looked at Bradley. "Why don't you tell Jackson what you overheard last week?"

"I was doing some filing, minding my own business, when Keith's dad entered the office. He and Keith look alike, you know. Like both of them should be king of the world." Bradley began to pick at his fingernails. "Then Dr. Kelsey asked me to get Keith. When I returned, they disappeared into Dr. Kelsey's office. Then the office ladies left for lunch."

"So you were alone?" Charlie asked.

Bradley nodded. "I went to the front desk and continued my filing. A few seconds later — after the air conditioner switched off — I heard voices coming through the vent above me."

Jackson wanted to hear more about the vent — how wide it was, what the vent plate screws looked like, how easy it would be for someone to climb through — but he pushed those thoughts aside. "What did they say?" he asked, pulling out his notebook and pencil.

"I didn't catch all of it. Something about putting Keith in the election even though the deadline had passed."

Jackson scribbled in his notebook. "Anything else?"

"Keith's dad said something about donating something to the school. Money, I think. Then Dr. Kelsey said something about winning no matter what." Bradley shrugged. "But I could be wrong about that last thing. The AC had just powered back on."

Charlie tapped the table. "Thanks, Bradley. That's all we need for now."

Bradley smiled as he slipped out of his chair. "It was nice to meet you, Jackson."

Still scribbling in his notebook, Jackson nodded in Bradley's direction. After Bradley left the library, he said, "That was good intel. I can't believe you didn't offer to pay him."

"I stopped him from ordering the chicken enchiladas the other day. He owes me."

"Sounds like a fair trade," Jackson said. "Can we trust him?"

"I think so," Charlie replied. "I don't have any reason to suspect he's lying."

Jackson rolled his pencil between his fingers as he stared at his notebook. "This is major, Charlie. If Kelsey really took a bribe to put Keith in the election, he could get into some serious trouble. Like, fired." He shrugged. "Too bad we don't have any proof."

"What about the bribe?"

"It'll look like a donation to the school." Jackson scratched through a few lines in his notebook. "There's one other possibility. Kelsey might not be in on this."

Charlie snorted. "Yeah, right."

"According to Mr. Pritchard, Kelsey has the right to allow someone else to run if there's only one candidate," Jackson said. "He might not know that Keith bribed Stewart to drop out. And as crazy as it sounds, Mr.

Sinclair's donation could be just that — an ill-timed donation."

"But Bradley said he heard Kelsey promise Keith a victory — no matter what."

"He heard *something* like that. Kelsey could have just been pumping Keith up, telling him that he could win no matter what type of campaign Gaby ran."

"Come on," Charlie muttered. "You can't believe that."

"No, but I can't disprove it either."

Charlie ran his fingers through his hair. "So now what?"

"While I want to believe Bradley, I need to find out for myself," Jackson said. "I have my weekly meeting with Dr. Kelsey tomorrow. I'll know once I talk to him."

He glanced at the wall. Keith had plastered huge, professionally made vinyl banners all over the school, telling students how great he was and why he should be president. They easily dwarfed all the other campaign posters.

Jackson sighed. "And I can't believe I'm saying this, but I need to talk to Keith."

THE **DEVIL** AND JACKSON GREENE

The next morning, as soon as Jackson entered the school, he headed toward Keith's usual hangout. Keith didn't look surprised to see him. "No sidekick today?" he asked. "Or did Speedy Gonzales finally grow a brain and figure out that he shouldn't cross me?"

Jackson balled his hands into fists. Even though he and Keith were about the same size, he could tell that Keith was puffing up his chest to look bigger. "That's not funny."

"Can't you take a joke?"

"You see me laughing?"

Keith picked up his book bag. "Come on. Too many ears around here. I think the doors to the science wing are unlocked."

Jackson hesitated before falling into step behind Keith. "FYI — Speedy Gonzales is Mexican, not Puerto Rican."

Keith kept walking, content to respond to Jackson with silence. As they crossed the atrium, Keith noticed a few of his classmates whispering as they passed. He wondered if they were talking about the Mid-Day PDA, or the Blitz at the Fitz, or the Shakedown at —

Idiot! Even *he* was using those stupid nicknames. Jackson Greene ruined everything, even his private thoughts.

But now, finally, he had one-upped Jackson. He had won. He had proven that he was a Sinclair after all.

Then he sneezed.

They entered the science wing and stopped outside of an empty classroom. Jackson brushed a petal from his jacket. "Allergies?"

Keith's eyes were starting to tear up, but he didn't want to draw attention to it. "It's not a good idea to annoy the next Student Council president, especially when I can destroy that garden of yours."

"How do you even have time to be president? I figured you'd be too busy buying off the competition with *Ultimate Fantasy IV.*"

"Aren't you supposed to be begging me to keep your garden funded?" Keith asked. "Or are you here to ask me to go easy on your girlfriend?"

"She's not my girlfriend."

Keith leaned against the wall. "And from the way it sounds, she never will be."

Jackson twirled his pencil between his fingers, taking in Keith's haughty smile and monogrammed shirt. "Why in the world do you want to be Student Council president? Did you suddenly develop a case of school spirit? Isn't it enough to be a starter on the basketball team and the —"

He stopped twirling. "What's the name of that fancy boarding school your brother attends?"

"The Winstead Academy. Ever heard of it?"

Jackson nodded. It was one of the many private schools his mother had threatened to ship him off to.

"Three generations of Sinclair men have attended the school," Keith said. "But they won't let just anyone in, even if you're a legacy student. You have to have impeccable grades, hundreds of hours of community service, and outstanding extracurricular activities. I've got basketball and debate and the Gamer Club on my résumé, but in order to seal the deal, I need to hold a position that shows leadership and responsibility and crap like that. And nothing looks better on an application than Student Council president."

"I can't believe you're doing this just to get into some snobby high school."

"It's not snobby. It's prestigious. And that's not the only reason I want to be president," Keith said with a smirk. "I promised the Gamer Club new AV equipment." He pushed himself off the wall. "I know who won't get any money — stupid Botany Clubs that plant stupid flowers that cause half the allergies in this school. The same with the Tech Club — wasting all that money on useless equipment."

"But how are they — we — supposed to get money?"

"Haven't you heard of bake sales?"

"If you want to be mad at me, fine. But don't take this out on the clubs. And don't take it out on Gaby."

"Look on the bright side — you can always join the Gamer Club." Keith checked the time on his phone. "I have to go. Got a lot of planning to do between now and the election. Have to get my acceptance speech — I mean, campaign speech — ready." He slipped his phone into his pocket. "I would tell you to call my cell if you wanted to discuss this more, but I almost forgot — you aren't allowed to carry one."

JACKSON and The MAN

Jackson entered the main office and headed to his usual seat, directly across from Dr. Kelsey's office. Unlike the main windows, which were one-way glass, the small windowpane in the principal's door was clear. Jackson could see Dr. Kelsey working at his desk. He figured he had at least fifteen minutes until Dr. Kelsey was ready for him. Keeping him waiting was one of Kelsey's "intimidation tactics."

So far, Jackson hadn't been intimidated.

He settled into his seat and balanced his book bag on his knees. Ms. Caroline Appleton — officially the school's senior administrative assistant, but old enough to remember when it was okay to be called a secretary — peered at Jackson over the rim of her glasses. "Are you here for your weekly meeting, or are you in trouble?" she asked. "Boys like you are always up to one thing or another."

Jackson looked at his skinny brown hands. He never quite knew what Ms. Appleton meant when she said "boys like you." He hoped she meant something like "boys named Jackson" or "boys who are tall," but he suspected her generalizations implied something else.

Mrs. Alicia Goldman, the other administrative assistant, turned down the volume on the small radio at her desk. "Hon, I'm sure he'll be ready for you any minute now. Want a piece of candy?"

"No, thank you." Jackson would have had a mouth full of cavities if he accepted candy from Mrs. Goldman every time he stepped inside the office.

She returned the butterscotch to the candy bowl before looking intently at the radio. Jackson saw that she was holding her breath as the song ended. The station cut to a commercial, and Mrs. Goldman lowered the volume even more.

"You won't win," Ms. Appleton said. "They never give those tickets to real people."

"Don't be so negative. There's still a chance. They haven't announced the winner yet." Mrs. Goldman eyed Jackson. "Do you know anyone with tickets to the Sk8tr Boiz concert? They were all sold out before I could buy them."

Jackson shook his head. The idea of Mrs. Goldman being a Sk8tr Boiz fan weirded him out. He figured someone like her — someone in her thirties — would like boring music, like smooth jazz.

The main door opened, and Marcelo Calderon walked in. As he handed Ms. Appleton a note, Jackson noticed that his eyes were puffy and his skin looked red.

"Sick, huh? Sure you're not faking it?" Ms. Appleton asked.

Marcelo shook his head. "My mom's coming to pick me up, but she can't get off until two. And the nurse had another patient, so she sent me here."

"So you can sit in here, getting everyone else sick? Great." She folded the note and slipped it into her cardigan pocket. "Can't one of your sisters or brothers pick you up? Or what about one of your cousins?"

"I'm an only child."

"Wasn't it you that had a whole boatload of people in here last week?"

No, Jackson thought. *That was Manuel Saenz.* Of course, at the time, Ms. Appleton had confused Manuel with someone else as well.

Jackson returned to staring at Dr. Kelsey's door. Actually, it wasn't the door that demanded his attention. Rather, the shiny, circular lock over the handle captured his gaze.

Jackson had heard about the Guttenbabel 4200 and its supposed unbreakability, but he hadn't encountered one until the day he and Katie Accord tried to break into Dr. Kelsey's office. The principal had confiscated Katie's cell phone, and Jackson had promised to get it back for her — for a small favor. "Piece of cake," he'd said.

Then he met the Guttenbabel.

He poked, pried, jimmied, shimmied, swore at, and shook the lock, using every trick he knew and a couple he made up. Nothing worked. He was still trying to crack it when he saw Dr. Kelsey, Keith, and a couple of Keith's minions approaching the main office door.

As Jackson looked at Katie, he realized Keith probably squealed to get even with both of them. Katie had dumped Keith two weeks earlier, the day after the Blitz at the Fitz. The day after he had tried to blame the blowout on her.

Just like that, Jackson knew how to one-up Keith.

So he kissed her. Or rather, he lightly brushed his lips against hers.

And Keith's face crumbled like a month-old cookie.

In the hour or two that followed, Jackson had actually been proud of himself. He hadn't been able to retrieve Katie's phone, but he had still won. Katie even offered to uphold her end of their deal — she had enjoyed the look on Keith's face as much as Jackson had. Sure, he'd lost a few privileges, but it could have been a lot worse. He hadn't lost anything *really* important.

And that's when Gaby stopped talking to him.

Fifteen minutes later, Dr. Kelsey cracked open his door. "I'm ready for you, Mr. Greene."

Jackson entered the small office and slipped into the worn seat in front of the desk. His file sat in the middle of the desk's otherwise empty surface, as it always did when he and Kelsey met.

Dr. Kelsey settled into his chair, folded his hands together, and stared at Jackson. Dr. Kelsey had seen enough television shows to know all about police intimidation tactics. Barricading himself in a room with a "suspect" made the guilty party feel that there was no way out. No escape. It caused them to say things that they normally wouldn't say. Although it hadn't yet worked with Jackson Greene, Dr. Kelsey always noticed how Jackson twisted in his chair and watched the door. He assumed it unnerved Jackson at least slightly, being in a room with an imposing authority figure such as himself.

"I talked to Mr. James this morning. He said you've been showing up earlier than usual this week." Dr. Kelsey usually found the security guard useless, but at least he had the common sense to note the comings and goings of Jackson Greene. "Anything you want to tell me?"

Jackson suppressed a groan. It was always the same routine. Kelsey spent ten minutes accusing Jackson of anything and everything that happened in the school over the past week. Then he sent Jackson to study hall, but not before waving the threat of expulsion in front of his nose.

Jackson usually spent most of the meeting wishing he was anywhere else. But today . . .

"Actually, yeah, I have something I'd like to talk about." He leaned forward. "What if I told you that a student involved with the election had violated the Honor Code?"

Dr. Kelsey arched one of his eyebrows. "Are you the student in question?"

Jackson shook his head. "I don't want to say anything more, but if you look closely, you might notice a few weird coincidences in the timing — who's gotten in and who quit." Even though he wanted Kelsey to investigate the Student Council elections, he didn't want to explicitly name Keith or Stewart or anyone else. *Rule Number Four: Never rat. No matter what.*

Dr. Kelsey flashed Jackson a toothy grin. "I know exactly what you're referring to," he said. "Keith gave a friend a gift, and on a totally unrelated note, this friend dropped out of the Student Council elections." He smoothed the few remaining hairs on his head. "The Sinclairs have always been charitable people. Why, Roderick Sinclair was in here just the other week, asking what the school needed, and I mentioned the new Umiliani espresso machine. . . ."

Jackson couldn't believe the principal had just volunteered all this information so . . . *smugly.* "You don't think people will consider Keith's gift a bribe?"

"I see it more like a donation."

Jackson closed his eyes for a few seconds as he took a long, deep breath. Kelsey was in on the whole thing.

"You should be glad that Keith is running for president," Dr. Kelsey continued. "He'll be a great leader for the school."

"What about Gaby? She'd make a great president too."

"I'm sure she would. That's why we have elections, so the student body can make the choice for themselves." He pulled at the lapels of his very snug jacket. "We have to honor the democratic process, after all. You never know what'll happen during an election."

After leaving Dr. Kelsey's office, Jackson took a slight detour on the way to study hall. As he walked, he reached into his jacket pocket and pulled out his notepad. It hadn't gotten much use over the last four months, but that was about to change.

Jackson stopped in front of Charlie's locker. On the paper, he wrote:

My house.
4:00 p.m.
I have a plan.

He slipped the note through a vent in the locker. Then Jackson let his eyes linger on one of Gaby's posters. He could still hear her voice in his head, asking why he kept breaking the rules. Asking why he couldn't keep his promise to be a normal student.

He placed his pencil behind his ear and straightened his tie.

Now wasn't a time to be normal. Now was a time to be infamous.

THE GREAT GREENE HEIST

Jackson sat in his kitchen, sipping hot Earl Grey tea while Charlie paced in a tight circle in front of him. He was glad they had the house to themselves, so his parents wouldn't see Charlie wearing a hole in their tiled floor.

Jackson finished his tea, then centered the cup and saucer on the table in front of him. "Thoughts?"

Charlie grabbed a handful of his hair and tugged hard. Jackson had just described the greatest heist in the history of Maplewood Middle School. A heist that not even Jackson's brother would have been brave enough to attempt. A heist destined to live in infamy — if they could pull it off.

Finally, Charlie said the truest thing he could utter. "You're crazy."

Jackson looked at the map of the main office on the table in front of them. "The plan has its challenges —"

"Challenges?" He jabbed at the drawing, his finger

landing on a small room at the rear of the main office. "How do you even know this layout is correct?"

"Samuel says so," Jackson said. "He's been back there, after all. And if it makes you feel better, we'll check it out before the election."

"Yeah, because I really want to break into the main office twice." Charlie pulled a chair from the table and sat down in front of Jackson. "We could just report Dr. Kelsey to the superintendent. I know we're not supposed to rat, but given the circumstances —"

"We don't have proof," Jackson said. "And as much as I want to take down Dr. Kelsey, our first priority has to be stopping Keith from winning the election."

Charlie nodded. "What does Samuel think about this plan of yours?"

Jackson ran his thumb along the edge of his saucer. He hadn't actually explained the *entire* plan to Samuel. "He said three weeks was tight —"

"I knew it!"

"Let me finish. He said three weeks was tight but doable . . . as long as we don't hit any major speed bumps."

Charlie shook his head. "You know there's no way we can pull this off alone."

"I know. We'll need a crew." Jackson opened his notebook and began flipping through the names he had jotted down during study hall. "There are a lot of students with a lot to lose if Keith becomes president. We just have to find people who won't spill."

"I'm guessing you want Hashemi for tech support."

"We are venturing where few have gone before."

Charlie winced at Jackson's *Star Trek* joke. "Hashemi couldn't finish a project if his life depended on it." He nibbled on his lip, then said, "We'd be better off with Megan —"

"No way."

"But —"

"Rule Number Nine: Loose lips sink ships," Jackson said. "Hashemi can handle it. He works great under pressure."

"I hope you're right." Charlie looked back at the map. "What about Bradley for an inside guy?"

"You trust him that much?"

"He hasn't let me down yet," Charlie said. "And we don't have many other options. Unless you want to consider Megan. . . ."

"Okay, I'm sold on Bradley." Jackson picked up his pencil. "The biggest problem we have is finding a bankroll. What about Quincy Scott?"

"Parents cut off his funds. Word on the street is he tried to steal his dad's Porsche and ended up driving it into the swimming pool."

Jackson scratched the name off the list. "Bettina Esquivel?"

"No good. She's got a huge crush on Wilton." Charlie leaned back. "What about Victor Cho? He's a member of the Chess Team, which needs money every year to attend the state finals. His parents are always traveling, which means they give him access to cash and credit cards. And he spent most of fifth grade running from Keith and

Wilton." He sat up. "Other than the fact that he's even more of a snob than Keith, he's perfect."

"And what about you?" Jackson shut his notebook. "Are you in?"

Charlie took in the drawing one last time. "You're still crazy," he said. "But yeah, of course I'm in. I'm your right-hand man."

THE **KOBAYASHI MARU**

On Friday, Hashemi Larijani found a folded, typewritten note between pages 122 and 123 of *The Unofficial Guide to the* Star Trek *Universe.*

At the same time, Victor Cho received a text from an unknown caller.

Two minutes later, as Bradley sat in computer class, an email from an anonymous sender popped into his inbox.

Each message contained the same three sentences:

Don't want Keith Sinclair to be
the next Student Council president?
Meet us at 5:00 p.m. at the shed
behind 421 Mockingbird Road.
P.S. Don't share this message with ANYONE.

While Bradley and Victor didn't recognize the address, Hashemi did. It was his house. And while he was a little upset with Jackson — at least, he assumed it was

Jackson — calling a meeting at his shed, he was also a little pumped up.

Okay, a lot pumped up.

Hashemi had never really been involved with one of Jackson's schemes before. Sure, he had served as an unofficial technical advisor from time to time — nothing major, just trivial input on things like how to anonymously sell livestock on eBay or remotely log in to the school server. Those missions were all hypothetical. Allegedly.

But he had never been summoned to a meeting before — had never gone with "the away team." He just hoped he wouldn't end up being a redshirt.

Hashemi got home well before the meeting so he'd have time to hide some of his more prized memorabilia — namely, the life-sized cutout of Seven of Nine from *Star Trek: Voyager*. He had just rearranged his action figures again when a small, wiry boy entered the shed.

"I'm Bradley Boardman." He looked around. "Did you call this meeting?"

Hashemi shook his head. "I imagine Jackson will show up at some point."

Bradley sat at one of the stools at the worktable. He pulled a small lump of clay from his pocket and began shaping it. "Mr. Jonas says we should always carry our medium around, just in case inspiration strikes," he said. "Easy for the guys that use chalk."

They both turned when they heard a knock.

Victor Cho stood at the entrance and rolled his eyes. As a member of the Chess Team, he didn't care for the more geeky members of the nerd spectrum — i.e., the Tech

Club, with their silly comic book talk and excessive "fan-boying" of electronics. He felt that they were beneath the more intellectual nerds.

"Did you organize this?" Victor demanded. "Because if so, I —"

"I didn't call the meeting. And it's not even five o'clock yet," Hashemi said. "You're welcome to read one of my comic books to pass the time. Or I can pull out the hand-held video game console I built. It's in beta, but —"

"No, thank you." Victor sat down at the table, opened his book bag, and pulled out a brand-new, barely read copy of *War and Peace*. "I have better things to do."

Hashemi chuckled. There was nothing better than riling up one of the Chess Team guys.

While Victor pretended to read Tolstoy, Hashemi watched Bradley mold his clay into various shapes. Bradley was putting the finishing touches on a pointy Vulcan ear-lobe when Hashemi's phone beeped.

Five o'clock.

Before the last beep had sounded, Jackson and Charlie entered the shed and joined them at the table.

Jackson slid his loosened tie back up to his neck. "Gentlemen, glad you could make it."

Victor closed his book. "Do you mind telling us what this is about? I missed an important Chess Team practice today."

Jackson sized up Victor Cho — the fancy watch too big for his wrist, the designer glasses like all the other rich kids at school, the grating voice that squeaked more than boomed. He hadn't been sold when he and Charlie talked yesterday, but with one look at Victor, Jackson knew they had picked the right guy.

"Just being curious," Jackson began, "but how much does it cost to take the entire Chess Team to the state finals?"

Victor shrugged. "I don't know. Mary Alice is the president. She and Mr. Bacote take care of the money stuff."

Charlie leaned forward. "The Chess Team gets its funding from Student Council. So does the Tech Club. And the Art Geeks. And every other organization. So if Keith Sinclair becomes president, he doesn't just control Student Council. He will essentially control every non-sport student activity."

Charlie quickly explained the bylaws situation. Jackson watched as the boys' faces switched from confusion to shock to horror.

Bradley, who was still trying to get over being invited to a secret meeting with all these cool people, raised his hand.

Jackson nodded at him. "We're not in class, Bradley."

Bradley looked up at his hand, then yanked it back down. "So what are we supposed to do? Throw the election?"

Two equally large grins spread across Jackson and Charlie's faces. "That's exactly what we're going to do," Jackson said.

"But how?" Bradley asked. "And what if we get caught?"

"We won't get caught," Charlie said. "Not if we're smart. Not if we stick to the plan."

Jackson could see the doubt etched on the boys' faces. "Either we do nothing and let Keith ruin each and every club that we belong to," he said, "or we make a stand."

"But the election is in three weeks," Bradley said.

"That's plenty of time," Jackson said, ignoring the scowl on Charlie's face.

Victor cleared his throat. "Maybe it would help if you explained the plan."

Jackson turned to Hashemi. "What's that old *Star Trek* movie you made me watch last year? The one where Spock dies —"

"*Star Trek II: The Wrath of Khan!*" Hashemi yelled. "It's, like, the best *Star Trek* movie ever. Much better than that rebooted piece of —"

"We get the point," Jackson said. "Why don't you tell the guys about the Kobayashi Maru?"

Hashemi bounced in his seat. "The Kobayashi Maru is a test of character. A computer presents the Star Fleet cadet with a simulated no-win scenario. Lieutenant Savik takes the test at the beginning of the movie. Because there's no way to win, she fails."

"She fails?" Bradley mumbled. This wasn't the pep talk he was expecting.

Jackson removed his pencil from behind his ear and tapped the table. "Refresh my memory — does anyone figure out how to beat the test?"

"Well . . . Captain Kirk does, kind of. He rigs the computer so a win is possible."

"You mean he cheats," Victor said.

"I guess you can say he cheats, but that depends on who you ask," Hashemi said. "From Captain Kirk's point of view, he wasn't cheating. He just changed the parameters of the test." Hashemi straightened his glasses. "Kirk doesn't believe in the no-win scenario."

"Neither do I," Jackson said. "So that's what we're going to do. We're going to rig the election."

TaG TEAM

While Jackson and his new crew talked over their plan, Gaby sat at Omar's dining room table, pecking away at her calculator. On the floor behind her, Lynne and Omar argued over the wording for a poster. They had been working for over an hour, but Gaby still hadn't grown comfortable in Omar's house, with its throne-sized chairs and antique oak table. There was no way her mother would have let her work in a space like this, but Omar's mom didn't bat an eye when they set up shop in the dining room.

Gaby jotted her newest computation on a legal pad and sighed, which made Omar and Lynne stop their argument. "Based on my calculations, the budget will cover new computers in the library, but it won't subsidize the organic food station," Gaby said.

Lynne stuck out her tongue. "Good. No one wanted to eat all that rabbit food anyway."

Omar shook his head as he retraced Gaby's name on

his large white poster. "I bet a lot of kids would like a more diverse food selection."

"Who? Carmen Cleaver and the animal squad?"

"The Environmental Action Team members are still voters," Omar said.

"So are the, like, four hundred students who like a piece of bacon every now and then," Lynne said. "And believe me, they won't get excited about some extra lettuce and radishes on a cart."

Gaby snapped her fingers. "Where's the budget from last year?" She began leafing through loose papers in a manila folder. "Maybe I can increase the Botany Club's budget and convince them to grow some vegetables. It won't be enough produce for the entire school, but maybe it'll be enough for the students who care."

Lynne grabbed her container of glitter. "If you're looking to spend money, how about buying the basketball team some new uniforms?"

"We just got new uniforms." Gaby continued to look through her paperwork. "If they can grow all those flowers with the little bit of funding they received last year, think what they could do if we triple their budget." She paused to jot herself a note. "I really need to set up a meeting with them."

Omar scratched a dry patch of skin on his elbow. "Um . . . Are you sure that's a good idea?" he asked. "A lot of people — not me, of course, but others — blame the Botany Club for the increase in allergies this year. Maybe we should talk this over a little more. Do a poll. We don't want to make a rash decision."

"They're wrong," Gaby replied. "According to Charlie, it's the cedar trees by the football field that cause the allergies." She abandoned her search for last year's budget. "I just hope there's enough money left over after the computers."

"Take money from another club. I'm sure that's what Keith would do." Lynne placed her poster on the table, on top of the one Omar had decorated a few moments before. "What do you think?"

Gaby leaned over and glanced at the poster. Her name took up the majority of the board, each letter sparkling in silver and gold. "It's nice, but you didn't include any of the campaign slogans."

"I ran out of room."

"Maybe you can fix it this weekend," Omar said, rising from the floor. "It's getting late. . . ."

"Oh, yeah. Right." Lynne smiled. "I need to head home."

"I'll leave with you. I'm almost —"

"No, it's okay," Lynne said. She patted Gaby's shoulder. "You stay here."

Gaby frowned. "What's going on?"

"Nothing." She grabbed her bag, then held her hand up like it was a phone. *Call me tonight,* she mouthed as Omar led her to the door.

Gaby sighed as she began to pack her bag. She may not have been as good at reading people as Jackson, but even she knew what was about to happen.

Omar returned a minute later with a white candy box in his hand. He cleared his throat a few times, but didn't speak. Gaby tried to make eye contact with him, but he seemed intent on looking anywhere but at her.

Finally, she asked, "Are you okay?"

He nodded, then took a deep breath. "Do you have a minute? There's something important I'd like to ask you."

THE SETUP

On Saturday morning, John Parson, the main office student helper, received a visit from Charlie de la Cruz. Two days later, John informed Ms. Appleton that due to his studies, he regretfully needed to take a break from being a fourth period office helper for the next three weeks.

Bradley Boardman just happened to take the scenic route through the office that day, and just happened to overhear John talking to Ms. Appleton. Bradley, out of the kindness of his heart, stepped forward and offered to serve double duty in both the guidance office and the main office during fourth period. He hadn't discussed this with the guidance office staff yet, but he was sure they would understand. The main office *needed* a student helper to ensure seamless communication between the students, faculty, and staff. As the guidance office would later attest, Bradley was a model student. Dependable. Trustworthy.

Ms. Appleton agreed: He was the perfect guy for the job.

A few hours later, Charlie caught up with Jackson at his locker. "We made the switch. All it took was a copy of *Uncanny X-Men* 266."

Jackson swung his locker open. "Did Victor balk at the price?"

"Of course." Charlie watched as Jackson began to empty his book bag. "Everything set for tomorrow?"

"Done. As long as they don't change the menu," Jackson said. "What about tonight?"

"After Mom's schedule *magically* cleared up, it was a piece of cake convincing her to visit my *tia* in Toledo for a couple of days. And according to Lynne, she and Gaby are definitely going to watch Omar play at the Fitz this afternoon." Charlie caught the flash of a scowl across Jackson's face. "Have you heard about Omar and Gaby and the dance?"

Jackson tapped on the cold metal locker door. "Found out this morning. Heard he even brought her a gift."

"Yeah. Chocolate-covered nuts."

Jackson's nose wrinkled. "I bet you twenty dollars she trashed them as soon as she got the chance."

She had actually passed them on to Charlie. "Dude, why don't you just tell her —"

"No."

"Jackson."

"I'm not telling her," Jackson said as he shoved another book into the locker.

Charlie readjusted his book bag strap. "Have it your way."

"So I'll be over at your place around four," Jackson

continued. "That'll give us at least a couple of hours to move everything."

For the first time since Jackson laid out his plan, Charlie stopped to think about what they were about to do. Now that they were in the execution phase, things seemed a lot more real. "Are you sure this is going to work?"

"Don't worry. By the time she notices tomorrow morning, you'll be long gone."

"No, I'm talking about the entire plan." He started counting off. "A Kobayashi Maru, a Carrie Nation, an Anakin Skywalker, a Windows Vista, and a Denver Boot paired with a White Rabbit and a Fallout Shelter. That's seven schemes in less than three weeks."

Jackson closed his locker. "Please don't tell me you spent all weekend making up names."

He shrugged. "I was inspired. *Ocean's Eleven* came on last night."

"Trust me, Charlie. The plan is solid." Jackson grinned. "Have I ever let you down?"

Charlie crossed his arms.

"Don't look at me like that. Your eyebrows grew back. Eventually." He began to walk away, but stopped once he noticed that Charlie hadn't moved. "What?"

"Hashemi asked me to talk to you —"

"Since when did you and Hash become best buds?"

"We're not. But still —"

"No, Charlie. We can't risk it."

"We have to tell her, Jackson. There's no way Megan would hang out with Stewart if she knew Keith gave him the video game." Charlie glanced at the election poster across from Jackson's locker. "Dude . . . What if it were Gaby?"

He groaned. "Okay. Fine. But it has to be anonymous. Megan can't know we tipped her off." Jackson tucked his empty book bag under his arm. "You know that was a low blow, right? Bringing Gaby into it? Think she'll slam the door in my face this time?"

"What do *you* think?"

Jackson rubbed his nose. "Okay. Let's plan to meet her outside. Away from the front door."

ONE-ON-ONE

Gaby followed Lynne up the rickety bleachers at Fitzgerald Park. "I can't believe I'm here," she said. "I have better things to do than watch boys play basketball. They aren't even that good."

Lynne brushed a few cigarette butts from the bleachers before sitting down. "You promised you wouldn't complain."

"I'm not complaining. I'm telling the truth. Plus, I don't want Omar to get the wrong idea about how I feel about him. I've already complicated things by agreeing to go to the formal with him."

"You hugged him, Gaby. You gave him a public display of affection. What idea was he supposed to get?"

"It wasn't a real hug. More like a quick, sideways shoulder pat."

Lynne tugged on her friend's hair. "You know who you sound like, right?"

That shut Gaby up.

It had taken Omar a few minutes of stuttering and stammering that Friday afternoon, but eventually he had asked her to the formal. And Gaby said yes because . . . Well, because she didn't want to hurt his feelings. He had done such a good job with her campaign, and he was a nice guy. Considerate and friendly. There were worse people to attend the formal with.

Then he asked her to come watch him play at the Fitz. She found herself saying yes again, because really, after all his help with the election, the least she could do was give up a few hours of her time to watch him play basketball.

But now that she was actually in the stands, with the sun beating down on her and time seemingly standing still, she wished she had had the courage — or at least the common sense — to say no.

She and Lynne weren't the only students braving the bright sun and humid afternoon weather. Kids lined both sides of the blacktop, with the high schoolers at the newer, fancier court. While some kids waited for their chance to play, most were spectators.

"There's Omar!" Lynne said, gripping Gaby's arm, her voice high and fake flirty. "Isn't he cute?"

"Yeah. Cute," Gaby said, though her mind had drifted from September to May, when Omar was the spectator and she was the one on the court here. She could still feel the sting of the ball against her palms as she caught Jackson's pass, could still hear the roar of the crowd as she elevated for the final shot over Keith, could still see the grin on Jackson's face as they walked off, victorious.

"You're thinking about the Blitz at the Fitz, aren't you?" Lynne asked.

"No, I —" Gaby couldn't help but grin herself. She would never admit it, but she was the one who had come up with that nickname. "That was a great game. . . . Even though I shouldn't have let Jackson run up the score."

"Everyone thinks Jackson cheated."

"But he didn't," Gaby replied. "And everyone doesn't think that. Only Keith."

"Enough about that." Lynne reached into her purse and pulled out a compact mirror. "We should be talking about your dress for the formal. Have you gone shopping yet?"

"I'll just wear something from last year."

"Like you can even fit into something from last year. You've grown at least two inches." Lynne looked at Gaby over the open mirror. "What's the point of donating all those clothes if you aren't going to buy new ones?"

"Well, at least now my favorite pair of jeans isn't too long." She glanced at her phone. "This is the slowest game in the history of the universe!"

"I don't understand you," Lynne said, snapping the compact shut. "You're supposed to *want* to watch Omar play. If you didn't want to come, you should have just said no."

"I know. I chickened out."

"Well, you'd better start thinking up some good excuses. He's planning to ask if you want to shoot hoops at your house tomorrow."

"Great. I'm going to have to pretend to be bad, just so I won't embarrass him."

"Or, you know, you could just say no. Or just beat him."

"But —"

"Look! He stole the ball!"

Gaby watched as Omar raced down the court and pulled up for a three. She shook her head. "He's a center. Why is he shooting a three when he can go in for a layup?"

"You're not supposed to criticize your boyfriend."

She cut her eyes at Lynne. "He is not my boyfriend."

"He could be, if you wanted one."

"Well, I don't want one."

"Sure. Right."

Gaby nudged Lynne in the ribs. "What does that mean?"

"Ouch!" Lynne rubbed her side. "It means you're still crazy about a boy who likes kissing other girls."

"No, I'm not!" Gaby said. Then after a few minutes she said, "And according to Jackson, it wasn't really a kiss. . . . More like a slight brushing of his lips against hers."

Lynne's mouth dropped open as she stared at Gaby.

"Ugh," Gaby said, burying her head in her hands. "I'm pathetic, aren't I?"

"Yeah, you are." Lynne squeezed her shoulders. "But at least you can be pathetic and look cute at the same time. So let's talk about that dress."

It was almost six o'clock by the time Gaby left the park. They had stayed to watch Omar play in two pickup games, each more mistake-filled than the last. Afterward, he jogged over and asked if Gaby wanted to play some one-on-one tomorrow. She said yes. Then, while he was talking to some of the high school boys, she pried Lynne away from the bleachers and headed home.

She didn't understand Lynne. As good of an athlete as she was, she seemed to be happiest when she was watching other people play. Well, not other people. Boys. Gaby promised herself that she'd never be like that.

But even as she did, she found herself thinking about last year's Fall Formal. Up until then, Gaby had never worn her hair in anything other than a ponytail, and the only makeup she owned was cherry-flavored Chapstick. But on the weekend before the Fall Formal, her aunt had popped into town to surprise Gaby with an all-day spa visit and makeover. Gaby had resisted — she wasn't girly like *Tia* Isabel — but she relented after seeing the hurt on her aunt's face.

The day had been exhausting. They started their morning in a spa, their faces covered in mud and cucumbers. At the salon, the hairdresser trimmed, chopped, and styled; washed, rinsed, and conditioned; and transformed Gaby's beautiful, practical, functional ponytail into a layered bob. Her aunt was so impressed, she bought three extra bottles of the salon's shampoo and conditioner.

They spent the next few hours at seemingly every makeup counter in Easton Town Center, painting Gaby's face a wide assortment of colors and shades. By the time they returned home, all Gaby wanted to do was barricade herself in the bathroom and peel the makeup off her cheeks. All that stood between her and clean pores were the two boys watching music videos in the den.

Charlie dropped the remote and feigned shock. "Who are you, and what did you do with my sister?"

"Shut up, Carlito," Gaby said, trying to sound like her mother.

"Wow."

Jackson rose from the couch and tucked his dangling arms behind his back. Forever Young, last year's "it" boy band, blared away on the television, but Jackson's eyes were focused on Gaby.

"I like it," he said. "You look . . . wow."

Charlie wandered over to his sister. "Man, your hair is shiny." He started to reach for it, but she stepped out of his grasp. "I won't mess it up!" He reached again and took a few strands in his hand. "Jackson, come feel this stuff."

Jackson crossed the room, his eyes still on Gaby. He stopped a few inches away from her — close enough for Gaby to smell her mother's *pasteles* on his breath — and slowly, he ran his fingers against her hair.

"Soft." He smiled at Gaby, but this was a new smile. A different smile. A smile as soft as clouds and cotton candy and everything sweet in the world. His hand brushed against a small red chrysanthemum that one of the stylists had tucked into her hair. "You look really . . . wow."

A year later, most of the makeup that Gaby's aunt had purchased remained unopened, and once Gaby's hair grew back out, she returned to her ponytail. But she always washed her hair with the special shampoo and conditioner.

When a certain boy came over to play video games with Charlie, she washed her hair twice, just to make it extra shiny. Extra soft.

So Gaby had to fight the urge to touch her hair when she saw Jackson and Charlie in the driveway. They were huddled together and their backs were to her, but she had no interest in trying to see what they were up to. As she jumped off her bike and wheeled it past them into the garage, she reminded herself that it was Jackson's fault that she was now attending the formal with Omar.

She returned to the driveway once she heard the familiar sound of a basketball against concrete. Charlie was sloppily dribbling the ball. He pulled up a few feet away from Jackson and launched the basketball toward the rim. It exploded against the backboard and bounced into the street.

"I'll get it," Jackson said.

"Since when do you play basketball?" she asked Charlie. Much to the disappointment of their father, her brother's usual idea of exercise was mashing buttons on his video game controller.

"It was Jackson's idea," he said. "He heard about you going to the Fitz."

Gaby watched as Jackson chased down the ball. "Who's winning?" she asked as she reached for her hair. She almost pulled it out of its ponytail, but stopped herself.

"Who do you think?" He shook his head. "Why don't you play with him?"

"Me? No, I . . . No, Charlie. No."

"Why not?"

"Because I don't want anything to do with Jackson Greene."

"Yeah. Right," he said, in the same tone that Lynne had used earlier. "You know you two —"

"Shut up," she hissed. "He might hear you."

They both stopped talking as Jackson ambled up the driveway, the ball nestled underneath his arm. "Hey, Gaby," he said.

Gaby crossed her arms. "Hello, Jackson."

Jackson looked at Charlie. "Ready to go again?"

"No way. Why don't you play with Gaby?"

"Charlie!" She shook her head. "I can't —"

"It's okay." A small smile crept across Jackson's face. "I understand."

"What's so funny?"

"Nothing." Jackson's smile grew. "After spending all afternoon watching other people play basketball, I can see how you're tired."

Gaby huffed. "I'm not tired."

"So you're scared?"

"Stop trying to goad me, Jackson Greene. It won't work."

Jackson dribbled the basketball, then threw it to her. By the time she realized he was passing it, she had already caught it.

"Come on," he said. "One game of HORSE."

Gaby looked at the basketball. She was supposed to be mad. Furious, even.

But Jackson also knew how to play basketball. He was taller and quicker, but she was a better shooter. She wouldn't have to pretend to be bad.

She rotated the ball in her hands, then took a shot. All net.

She chased down the ball as it rolled into the street. "Where's Charlie?" she asked when she returned to the driveway.

Jackson pointed at the house. The window curtain jerked shut.

"Just so you know, I'm still mad." She passed the ball. "Furious, even."

"I figured." He dribbled the ball between his legs.

He was so much better than Omar at that.

Jackson and Gaby traded shot after shot, neither speaking. Gaby was working up a sweat, and she could see that Jackson was as well. It was like things used to be — before fancy shampoos and ill-advised kisses and lukewarm hugs.

After Gaby won the game, she asked, "Now what?"

Jackson shrugged. "Round two?"

"Okay." She tossed the ball to Jackson. "But enough HORSE. Let's play for real. Let's play one-on-one."

Two hours later, they finally stopped playing, but only because it was too dark to see. Had Gaby's mother been home, she would have called Gaby in an hour ago. But Mr. de la Cruz thought his daughter should always have a basketball in her hands.

They collapsed in the grass, both of them exhausted, each taking swigs from bottled water. Jackson wasn't sure which of them had won more games — he was having too much fun to keep track. He finished off his water and screwed the cap back on. "I heard about you and Omar."

Gaby took an extra-long drink from her bottle.

"He's in my English class," Jackson continued. "He's . . . nice. It takes him forever to pick a topic when we're writing essays, but he's nice." He tapped the bottle against the ground. "Is he your boyfriend or something?"

"We're just friends."

"Oh."

Gaby waited for Jackson to continue, but he just kept opening and closing his empty water bottle. Finally, she asked, "So are you going to the formal with Katie?"

He shook his head. "I haven't talked to her since the end of last year." He nudged the basketball with his feet, pushing it into the driveway. "I never liked her like that."

Gaby frowned. "Then why did you do it?"

"It's complicated," he said as he stood up. He reached out to help her up, but she waved him off as she rose to her feet.

"You owe me a better explanation than that," she said. For three days straight, that kiss was all people had talked about at school, over and over and over again. "Just tell me why you *kissed* her." Gaby hated even saying the word.

Jackson pinned the basketball between his feet. "Keith ratted me out. It was the only way I could get back at him." He shrugged. "It was a gut reaction."

"Well, that's just brilliant!" Gaby bent down and grabbed the ball. She dribbled it a few times, pounding it into the concrete. "Why did you even sneak into the office with her? Why didn't you go in with someone else, like Charlie?" *Or like me,* she wanted to add.

"Katie and I made a deal." Jackson went for the ball, but Gaby refused to give it to him. "I had a good reason."

"But you won't tell me what it is."

"You wouldn't understand." He shoved his hands in his pockets. "You'll think it's stupid."

From Jackson's point of view, he indeed had a good reason for the Kelsey Job. The Mid-Day PDA. The slight, insignificant brushing of his lips against Katie Accord's.

But Jackson was a boy.

And Gaby was a girl.

And there were some things that thirteen-year-old boys didn't tell thirteen-year-old girls.

Gaby and Jackson didn't speak for a few moments. After she yawned, he said, "I guess I should go." He took a step toward her. "Thanks."

She stopped dribbling. "For what?"

"For not slamming a door in my face this time."

Gaby couldn't help it. She smiled. But only a little.

"Hey — I hear they're serving meat loaf for lunch tomorrow."

She stuck out her tongue. "Yuck! I hate —"

"I know. Tomorrow might be a good day to pack your lunch."

She nodded. She wanted to say more, to say something, to say *anything*, but the words got lost between her brain and her mouth.

The screen door swung open, and Charlie stepped outside, carrying Jackson's book bag. "Your dad called."

Jackson took the bag. "Tell him I'm heading home now." Once Charlie disappeared into the house again, Jackson turned to Gaby. "Look, whatever happens, I want you to know . . ." He adjusted the straps. "I learned my lesson with the Kelsey Job."

"What does that mean?" Gaby asked.

"I'm going to keep my promise about following the rules and staying out of trouble." He began to back away. "Mostly."

"Jackson . . ."

He had already reached the street. "Good night, Gaby." His face was barely visible. "See you tomorrow."

Gaby spun the ball before sinking one last jumper. "Good night, Jackson Greene."

OFF THE RACK

Gaby's alarm clock rang much too loudly and much too late the following morning. As she sprinted to the shower, she replayed the events of the night before, trying to remember why she had reset her alarm clock (not that she even remembered doing this). The pickup game with Jackson had worn her out more than she had realized. She had barely been able to stay awake as she finished her homework, and just when she was about to slink off to the shower, Omar texted. She had felt obligated to write back, though Omar did the majority of the texting, while she replied with a halfhearted yes/no/maybe every few minutes. She hadn't even realized she had fallen asleep until her alarm clock jarred her awake, her cell phone on the pillow beside her.

Standing in the shower, Gaby found her mind floating back to the pickup game with Jackson. To the way he congratulated her at the end of every game, no matter the outcome (she won twice, lost once). To the way his skin felt when he handed her the ball. To the steadiness in his voice when he reminded her of his promise.

Gaby stuck her head underneath the showerhead, soaking her hair. Running for president against Keith was hard enough. Why did everything else have to be so confusing?

Once out of the shower, she toweled off and went to the medicine cabinet to get her contacts. That's when she noticed the message in the foggy mirror.

GABY —
ALL YOUR POSTERS ARE MADE FROM 100%
RECYCLED MATERIAL.
— C.

She rolled her eyes as she wiped the mirror clean. Charlie clearly had too much free time on his hands.

She had totally forgotten about the note by the time she returned to her bedroom. She pulled her hair into a ponytail, then opened her closet door.

It was empty.

All her dresses were gone. All her favorite shirts and sweaters. The skirts she wore to mass. The nice pants she wore on game days. Only a puke-green T-shirt and a ratty pair of jeans remained on the rack.

A small note was pinned to the jeans.

KEITH'S BANNERS ARE MADE FROM VINYL.
MUCH MORE DIFFICULT TO RECYCLE

THAN YOUR BOARDS.
P.S. I'M SORRY.

She ran to her dresser and started yanking open drawers. Every T-shirt and pair of jeans and shorts had been removed.

Gaby grabbed her robe, quickly knotted it around her waist, and marched to her brother's room. She burst through the door and found another message on the bed.

HIS BANNERS AREN'T EVEN LABELED WITH
RESIN ID CODES.

Gaby ripped the message in half, then went through *Charlie's* closet and dresser drawers.

No shirts. No shorts. Nothing.

Gaby wanted to scream. She went to her parents' door, but paused before knocking. Her mother was still in Toledo, and as mad as she was, she didn't want to wake her father. He was a fireman and had a long shift ahead of him.

Gaby returned to her room and picked up the T-shirt. It was only then that she noticed the logo on the front.

This wasn't even her shirt.

It was a Sk8tr Boiz shirt. She *hated* the Sk8tr Boiz.

But she had nothing else to wear.

So Gaby counted to ten, then twenty. Then thirty.

And only then did she slip on the T-shirt.

She quickly finished getting dressed and grabbed her book bag (at least Charlie hadn't taken that). It wasn't until she was standing outside, about to shut the back door, that she noticed the open loaf of bread and the mustard container on the counter.

She marched back into the kitchen. She couldn't believe her brother was such a slob, but at least the food had reminded her that she needed to pack a lunch. She glanced at the clock — just enough time to throw together a sandwich. She opened the refrigerator to grab the lunch meat.

All gone.

Gaby crushed the empty turkey container and slammed it into the trash can, pretending it was Charlie's face.

She thought about buying the school lunch, but the cafeteria meat loaf wasn't much better than the chicken enchiladas. She could have taken the last of the tortilla soup from last night's dinner, but she didn't have a way to heat it up at school. Plus, she was sure her father planned to eat it for lunch.

So she grabbed a cup of yogurt and an apple, and fixed herself a cheese sandwich.

The lunch of champions.

Lucky for Charlie, he managed to avoid Gaby all morning. She intended to continue her search for him as soon as she finished lunch, as she was planning on literally ripping the shirt from his back. Whatever he was wearing, it had to be better than her Sk8tr Boiz T-shirt.

Gaby had just settled into her seat in the cafeteria when Carmen Cleaver sat down across from her. "Nice T-shirt," Carmen said. "I've got three of them. Their music sounds like crap, but the profits from every shirt sold goes to People for the Ethical Treatment of Animals."

Gaby paused, her cheese sandwich inches from her mouth. Even though Carmen had been a student at Maplewood since sixth grade, Gaby didn't know her very well. To be honest, Gaby avoided her. Carmen wasn't necessarily mean, but she didn't have much of a filter.

Gaby caught sight of Lynne and Fiona standing by a nearby table. There was no way they were coming to join Gaby and Carmen — not with meat loaf on their trays. Carmen was a militant vegetarian.

"I have to admit, I was a little surprised when Jackson asked the Environmental Action Team to support your campaign," Carmen said. "Not that we're fans of Keith Sinclair — but both of you have similar campaign slogans. And both of you use too many printed materials."

Gaby thought back to the note on the mirror. "All of my posters are made from one hundred percent recycled material."

"That's what Jackson said." She sighed. "That's at least better than Keith. He had the nerve to plaster those hideous vinyl banners all over the school."

"Um . . . Are they labeled with resin identification codes?" Gaby asked, even though she already knew the answer.

"No! Which will make them even harder to recycle." Carmen pulled a folder from her book bag. "When I confronted Keith about the banners, he promised they would be repurposed correctly and wouldn't end up in some landfill. But I'm like, if you really cared about the environment, you wouldn't have used them in the first place." Carmen pulled a sheet of paper from her folder. "Jackson showed me your plan to reduce paper waste. He warned me that it was a work in progress, but it's a good start."

"He did what?" Gaby dropped her sandwich. "Let me see that."

Gaby looked at the creased sheet of paper. This plan was a week old. *Where did Jackson get this from?*

Then it clicked. This was the version she had been working on in the library. The version she had shown to Jackson.

The version she had *thrown* at Jackson.

"Clearly, you have a lot of work to do," Carmen said. "No one in their right mind would add more Sloanbook computers to the school. That company is notorious for —"

"I know," Gaby said. "I've already replaced the Sloanbooks with a different brand. Sloanbooks are less expensive, but the company has a horrible greenhouse emissions record." She was glad this was a fact she had learned without Charlie's help. "Cheaper isn't always better, right?"

Carmen nodded. "Yeah, I don't know why —" She stopped as she noticed Gaby's cheese sandwich. "Are you going vegetarian?"

"I . . . um . . . no." She pushed her plate farther away. "It just looks like . . . . I don't think it's for me."

"Not everyone is strong enough to stick with the lifestyle. But at least you tried." She looked across the room toward Keith as he bit into his meat loaf. "Ugh. He doesn't even close his mouth when he chews."

Gaby snuck a glance at her watch. "Well, I should get going before —"

"I asked Keith for his updated campaign plan too," Carmen continued, her eyes still on Keith. "He said he was waiting until after the election to formalize it." She shook her head. "What a cop-out."

Gaby couldn't help but laugh. "Are you surprised?"

Carmen finally turned away from Keith. "Remember when his dad got that big award for cutting his company's carbon footprint?" Gaby didn't, but she nodded anyway. "During the ceremony, Mr. Sinclair gave this great quote: 'Our primary job as the leaders of today is to make a better tomorrow.'

"So the next day, I found Keith after lunch and asked if he would like to join the Environmental Action Team. Then I asked if his father would consider coming to one of our meetings."

Gaby's stomach knotted. She knew where this was heading.

"Keith laughed in my face," Carmen said. "'My dad doesn't care about the environment,' he said. 'That upgrade was just for the tax breaks.'"

Gaby shook her head. "I'm sorry."

"Keith finished his soda and threw the can in the trash, even though he was within arm's reach of a recycling bin. And then he stood there and watched as I fished the can out." Carmen looked at Gaby, her eyes clear and determined. "Anyway, when Jackson talked to me this morning, he called you 'the leader for tomorrow.' Maybe he really *is* good enough to know how to push my buttons, or maybe he just got lucky — either way, it reminded me of that article. It reminded me that words aren't enough. You and Keith may have the same campaign slogan, but you are clearly the better candidate." She slapped her hand on the table. "It's simple, really. If we get you elected, you'll help us save the environment. And then, the world."

Gaby pulled at her shirt collar. "Carmen, I'm honored, really. But you don't have to do anything outrageous. Having the vote of the Environmental Action Team is enough."

"We're not the Environmental Action Team anymore. Starting today, we're SAKS. Students Against Keith Sinclair." Carmen crossed her arms. "We'll blanket the school with posters. We'll hand out flyers. We'll even picket. I promise, we will do everything in our power to get you elected."

She slapped the table one last time. "And I mean *everything*."

Charlie leaned against the building and pulled at his hair as he watched Gaby storm across the quad toward him. He had already been barred from playing video games for a week for taking bets on the parish's volleyball team — allegedly. He had no clue what this latest act would cost him if Gaby decided to tell their parents.

"I'm sorry," he said as soon as she was within range.

"Not good enough, Charlie. What are you and Jackson up to?"

Charlie tugged on his hair again, making it look like a

bird's nest caught in the middle of a typhoon. As much as he wanted to, he couldn't tell Gaby about how Keith's father had bribed Dr. Kelsey. He and Jackson couldn't risk her dropping out of the election in protest. "I'm sorry, Gaby. But you're just too nice. If you're going to win, you need someone on your side who, as Jackson puts it, is simultaneously irritating and relentless."

"No one listens to Carmen."

"They will this time," Charlie said. "She's already been talking to the Art Geeks. They're thinking about molding a clay figurine of Keith dressed as a wolf in sheep's clothing."

"But I want to run a positive campaign."

"That's why you're not running it," he said. "SAKS is an independent organization of concerned students."

"Charlie —"

"Keith bribed Stewart into dropping out of the election. He got Kelsey to bend the rules to let him run. And he stole your campaign platform." Charlie pushed himself off the wall. "Is it really a smear campaign if we're telling the truth?"

Gaby chewed on her lip, then said, "You came up with SAKS, didn't you?"

"Like it? Not my finest work, but I was in a rush."

"Do you honestly think this will work? Keith's a bully, but he's still popular enough to get the sixth grade and jock vote. Based on Omar's calculations —"

"Forget about Omar's numbers. Just run your campaign. Me and Jackson will handle the rest."

"You and Jackson? What, there's more?" She planted her hands on her hips. "All I know is, my clothes better be back in my room —"

"*Oye,* they'll be there by the time you get home." He picked up his bike. "Stop by your locker. Jackson left you a gift."

"You know, instead of making me wear this hideous shirt, you could have just told me all those facts this morning."

Charlie smiled. "Jackson believes that actions speak louder than words."

After he pedaled off, Gaby headed to her locker. She spun the combination and opened the door. Inside was a plain black T-shirt . . .

Her favorite pair of jeans . . .

A Forever Young CD . . .

And a small, red chrysanthemum.

IT'S **NOT** a SPEED **BUMP**

If someone had asked Lincoln Miller to quote Article XXIII, Section B5 of the Student Council bylaws, he would have said that "in the event of questionable results, the ballots were to remain in the possession of the Student Council advisor until they could be hand-counted by the Maplewood Honor Board." Mr. Pritchard generally kept all of his important files in a tall gunmetal-gray cabinet in his classroom. The file cabinet was always locked, as was Mr. Pritchard's room after school hours.

Fortunately for Jackson Greene, locked doors and metal file cabinets posed little challenge to a boy with his particular skill set.

So as Jackson went over the plan again with Victor, Bradley, and Hashemi, he reiterated how simple it would be. The night before the election, they would sneak into the copy room — housed inside the main office — and swap out the old Scantron machine for a rigged one. Even if Kelsey replaced every ballot with one supporting Keith, the printout would show that Keith lost.

Keith, of course, would demand a recount. Then Jackson would slip into Mr. Pritchard's office over the weekend and replace enough of the ballots to tip the election in Gaby's favor.

Simple.

All Jackson had to do was create a bump key.

"And what exactly is a bump key?" Bradley asked, scratching dried paint from his fingertips.

Jackson retrieved the padlock from the shed door. "A bump key is a key with the teeth filed down to the lowest notch. It's the quickest way to pick a lock." He stuck a bronze key into the closed padlock, then tapped on the end of the key with a screwdriver. Two seconds later, the padlock popped open.

Hashemi cleaned his glasses with the edge of his untucked shirt. "Couldn't you have waited a few days before cracking another of my padlocks?"

Jackson smiled as he walked to a pegboard and slipped the key onto a hook. "It's easy to create a bump key. All you need to know is the type of lock, and voilà." He pointed to the array of keys on the pegboard. "I've already created bump keys for Mr. Pritchard's office and his file cabinet. And Bradley was kind enough to borrow a main office key for a few hours so I could create a bump key for it as well."

"And what about the copy room?" Victor asked.

"That's where things get a bit more complicated. Have any of you guys ever been inside the copy room?" Jackson waited for them to shake their heads, as he knew they would. "Up until a few years ago, students used to be allowed in the copy room. Then someone broke in one night and made photocopies of his . . . posterior."

"You mean someone named Samuel Greene," Charlie said, entering the shed.

"His name isn't important. What's important is that because of this unknown individual's actions, the school made the room off-limits to students, including office helpers." Jackson led his crew to the wooden door he had propped against the wall last week. "While most locks are made to look the same, if you look closely, you'll usually find the name of the manufacturer on the outside of the lock, below the keyhole." He knocked on the door, letting its hollow sound ring throughout the shed. "Unfortunately, this isn't the case for the lock to the copy room."

"Which means the manufacturer's name is etched either on the copy room side of the lock, or on the face-plate on the edge of the door, right below the deadbolt," Charlie added, slipping onto a stool.

Bradley scratched his head, getting pink paint flecks in his hair. "So . . . In order to break into the room, you need to figure out what type of lock it is. But in order to figure out what type of lock it is, you have to break into the room. . . ."

"A paradox," Hashemi said, staring at the door. "Just like in *Star Trek* episode 41, 'I, Mudd.'"

Jackson, trying his best not to laugh at Hashemi, stepped closer to Charlie. "So how is she?" he whispered. "Is she mad?"

"I'd avoid her for the next few days if I were you."

Jackson nodded. He had been avoiding Gaby for the last four months; he didn't know if he could stay out of her way any more than he already did.

Victor cleared his throat. "We have a huge problem — and you want to ask about some girl?" He shrugged at Charlie. "No offense."

"It's not a problem," Jackson said. "It's more of a snag." *And she's not some girl.*

"Not even a snag. A speed bump, really," Charlie added. *And she's not some girl.*

"Not even that," Jackson said. "Just a rock in the road. A speck of sand in the ocean. A —"

"Can't we just have the rigged machine delivered?" Hashemi asked. "That way, we don't have to break into the room. We can have someone do it for us."

Charlie and Jackson looked at each other. They weren't used to being surprised. "Good idea," Jackson said, "but we'd still have to get into the room to figure out what type of machine the school uses. You can't rig it if you don't know the type, right? But don't worry. I have a plan." He brushed a speck of dried paint from Bradley's shoulder. "Just being curious, Bradley — can you read upside down?"

OKAY, SO MAYBE IT IS

The next day during fourth period, Bradley stood a few feet away from the copy room, trying to blend into the shadows. He wiped his hands on his jeans for the third time in as many minutes and whispered Jackson's instructions to himself.

Be calm and be cool.

Bradley thought calm, cool thoughts as he listened to the copy machine roar behind the heavy wooden door. Mrs. Goldman had entered the room moments ago, carrying a small stack of papers.

Bradley pulled out the metallic, bricklike purple cell phone that Hashemi had slipped to him before school. While pretending to text (pretending because that function didn't currently work), Bradley took pictures of the copy room door, zooming in on the handle and the lock. Jackson had asked him to take as many photos as possible, just in case they needed more information.

He took a few more photos as the copy machine died down. Then, gripping the phone tightly in his hand, he positioned himself in front of the door and took a deep breath.

The lock jingled, then the door flew open. Bradley caught it inches before it slammed into his face. He blinked, amazed that he hadn't ended up with a broken nose. Then he remembered the plan.

"Ouch," he moaned, covering his nose and bending over.

"Who's that — Bradley? Are you okay? What are you doing back here?" He heard Mrs. Goldman speaking over him, but his gaze remained glued to the plate on the skinny edge of the door. It took a second, but his eyes found the words that Jackson said would be there.

"Bradley," Mrs. Goldman said again, her hand on his back. "Are you hurt?"

Bradley stood back up. "No, I'm okay," he said, his hand still covering his nose. "I was just trying to text my mom before —"

"Let me see."

For a second, Bradley thought she was talking about the phone. "No, it's —"

"Let me see," she repeated, prying Bradley's hands away from his face. "Hm . . . Your nose isn't red, but it does look a bit swollen."

Swollen? Bradley thought. *But the door didn't hit it!*

"Come on," she said. "Let's put a cold compress on it."

"I'm okay." He backed away. "It doesn't even hurt."

"Are you sure?" she asked, her eyes widening. "It's getting bigger as we speak."

Bradley reached for his nose again. "Really, I'm fine. I'll put some ice on it as soon as I get home."

"No," she said, taking him by the arm. "I insist."

As Bradley allowed himself to be dragged to the nurse's office, he repeated the name of the lock over and over in his head so he wouldn't forget it.

A Guttenbabel 4200.

Jackson would be so happy with him.

YOUR LUCKY DAY!

Jackson had always believed that Dr. Kelsey's office was the only room in the school secured with the Guttenbabel 4200. It was a double-barrel deadbolt, meaning it could be locked from either side of the door, and it employed a faint electrical current that made picking it virtually impossible. The lock was extremely expensive, and the majority of rooms at Maplewood didn't need that level of security. However, after an unnamed person plastered his "Seymour Butts for Homecoming King" posters around school, the district apparently felt it was in their best interest to update some of the locks.

Good-bye, crappy Ultra Lock. Hello, Guttenbabel 4200.

After learning the news, Jackson spent an hour or so feeling sorry for himself. Then he got to work. By that afternoon, he'd figured out a new plan.

"Just talk normal," Jackson said. He picked up the phone and offered it to Victor, but the other boy refused to take it. They sat alone in Hashemi's shed — Jackson had asked everyone else to wait outside. Jackson hoped that

Victor would feel more comfortable with fewer people around.

"Do I really have to do this?" Victor asked, staring at the cordless phone in Jackson's hand.

"Do you want to stop Keith or not?" Jackson leaned against the table. "How many times did he flush your homework down the toilet in elementary school?"

"Fourteen times. Sixteen if you count the extra credit."

"If he wins, the next thing he'll flush is the Chess Team," Jackson said. "Think about it this way — compared to what you have to do tomorrow, this is a walk in the park."

"Tomorrow? What happens tomorrow?"

Jackson quickly explained his plan. "I'd love to get one of the other guys to do it, but we have to do it during seventh period, when the main office will be its emptiest. That rules out Hash, because it's impossible to get him out of Mrs. Berry's class. And for obvious reasons, it can't be me or Charlie."

"But can't Bradley —"

"With all the paint he gets in his hair? They'd recognize him in an instant."

"I have money." Victor tried to stand. "Can't we just hire someone —"

Jackson pushed him back into his seat. "Focus, Victor. You can do this."

"But —"

"I'm dialing." Jackson punched the keypad with his index finger. "It's ringing."

Victor took the phone and pressed it against his ear.

"Hello. Hello?"

After a few seconds, Jackson nudged Victor.

"Hello . . . Mrs. Alicia Goldman?" he croaked. "This is Carson Baxter from WJXI. Congratulations — you've just won a pair of tickets to see the Sk8tr Boiz!"

THE FORGETTABLE VICTOR CHO

Caroline Appleton couldn't believe that Mrs. Goldman had called in sick. Ms. Appleton had been an administrative assistant at Maplewood for nearly thirty years, since Senator Maplewood himself was principal, and she had never missed a day of school. Not even when she had a fever of 102 degrees. Not even when she broke three fingers on her left hand. Not even when her dog died.

Mrs. Goldman blamed her sudden sickness on allergies, but Ms. Appleton figured it was somehow related to the Sk8tr Boiz concert taking place that evening in Cincinnati. While Ms. Appleton would never skip work to attend some teenybopper concert, she had to admit, those Sk8tr Boiz could belt out some catchy tunes.

She glanced at her watch as the seventh period bell rang. Like most of the students, she was more than ready for the day to be over. She started cleaning her desk in anticipation of leaving as soon as school ended.

She looked up as the office door swung open, and frowned at the sight of Jackson Greene. "What are you doing here? Didn't you already have your weekly meeting with Dr. Kelsey?"

Jackson nodded. "I know . . . but there's something I need to tell him."

"He's tied up on a conference call with the district superintendent."

Out of the corner of his eye, Jackson watched as Megan Feldman, the seventh period office helper, typed at a computer. The football team had an away game; she was already dressed in her cheerleader uniform. She glanced up, tucked a strand of hair behind her ear, and smiled. "Hi, Jackson."

Jackson stared back without blinking. Her smile faltered.

"Hello," he finally said. Then he turned toward Ms. Appleton. "I know Dr. Kelsey's busy, but it's important."

Ms. Appleton grunted as she picked up her phone and dialed. "Dr. Kelsey . . . Yes, I know who you're on the phone with. . . . Jackson Greene is in the office. He says it's important." She nodded, then hung up the phone. "He'll be out in a —"

Dr. Kelsey's office door flew open. "Mr. Greene! Why are you here?"

Jackson started to open his mouth, then paused. A nervous, worried, perplexed look washed over his face. "Maybe you should call Charlie in as well. I promise, it was all his idea."

Dr. Kelsey stepped forward. "What did you do?"

Jackson nibbled on his bottom lip, glanced at the wall

clock behind Ms. Appleton, then looked at the floor. "Again, I think you'd better get —"

"Megan, run and get Charlie de la Cruz out of class," Dr. Kelsey said. "Now, please."

"Sure," she said, rising from her desk. "Let me look up —"

"He's in Mr. Woodson's room." Dr. Kelsey stepped back into his office. "Come in, Mr. Greene."

It was only a few seconds after Megan exited the office that another student entered. His black horn-rimmed glasses covered half his face, and his hair looked as stiff as a football helmet. Ms. Appleton took his hall pass. "George Rhee. You were in here last week, right? Dr. Kelsey was giving you some award."

That had been Danny Nguyen — who was Vietnamese, not Korean — but "George" didn't correct her. "Mr. Jonas needs an extra pack of paper for art class," he said.

"Does this look like an art store?" Ms. Appleton grumbled. She wasn't fond of Mr. Jonas and all his newfangled "group learning" activities. As far as Ms. Appleton was concerned, the old ways of teaching kids worked just fine.

"I don't even like art that much," he said. "I'd rather take another math or science class, but the school board . . ."

"Don't get me started on the school board. How are we supposed to get our kids ready for the 'global marketplace' or whatever they call it if we're not cramming their schedules with math and science? I bet those Asians aren't wasting their time on art and music — no offense."

As she continued her rant, Victor — that is, "George" — glanced at the clock.

Ten seconds.

"Not to interrupt, but could I please get that paper?" he asked.

"Well, I suppose. But I plan to give Mr. Jonas a stern tongue-lashing about class preparedness," she said. "I need to —"

She stopped as her desk phone rang. "They can leave a —"

Then the phone on the office counter rang.

Then the familiar ringtone of the Sk8tr Boiz's "Eye M Sew N Luv" came from the bottom drawer of her desk.

The main office hadn't been this popular since the Mid-Day PDA.

Ms. Appleton sighed, letting her eyes linger on the hall pass. "You're a good kid," she said. "I suppose I can trust you." She pulled a set of keys from her pocket, pointed out a chipped bronze one, and handed him the key ring. "The supply closet is around the corner. The paper is on the third shelf."

Victor rounded the corner, holding every important key in Ms. Appleton's life — including the key to her twenty-two-year-old Ford Taurus, twelve scuffed bronze keys, and an oddly shaped, specially cut, shiny silver one.

When he returned with the ream of paper tucked underneath his arm, the phones in the office had stopped ringing. One call was a wrong number, the other was for Mrs. Goldman, and whoever called Ms. Appleton's cell phone had neglected to leave a message.

"Thank you," Victor said, dropping the keys into her outstretched palm.

Ms. Appleton quickly counted the keys. Satisfied, she said, "I see you found what you needed."

Instead of looking at the pack of pink paper, he glanced at the massive, bricklike cell phone in his hand. "Yes. I got exactly what I came for."

After Megan Feldman tracked down Charlie — it seemed that he had a bad stomachache and had spent the first few minutes of seventh period in the bathroom — he and Jackson Greene sat before Dr. Kelsey and told him the truth.

They believed the Botany Club should be able to plant flowers along the football field.

After Dr. Kelsey finally calmed down — he had hung up midsentence on the superintendent in order to talk to the boys — he spent the next hour grilling them, trying to coerce, trick, and manipulate them into confessing to at least some minor infraction. Jackson passed the time by counting the remaining hairs on Dr. Kelsey's head. Charlie entertained himself by silently humming the entire Sk8tr Boiz debut album.

By the time they were allowed to leave, the school was empty. They headed directly to the shed, where Hashemi was already at work transposing high-resolution photographs of a certain silver key into three-dimensional schematics.

Schematics that could create a key for a Guttenbabel 4200.

BEN AND ULYSSES CALL IN a FAVOR

The Saturday afternoon air was warm and muggy as Jackson and Charlie stepped off the bus at North High and Price. Although the neighborhood of Short North was filled with legitimate art galleries, restaurants, and coffee shops, if one knew where to look, one could always find a business of questionable intent.

Fighting the pull of fresh, hot doughnuts, Jackson and Charlie passed a bakery and entered Basilone's Lock and Key. The sign said that they were open, but the shop was empty. A thin layer of dust covered the various shelves and countertops, and the smell of burnt metal hung in the air.

"Hello?" Jackson called out. "Anyone here?"

"Coming," a voice said from behind a thick green curtain. "I'll be there —"

Jackson grinned as Ray Basilone appeared. Ray and Jackson's brother had been best friends all through middle school and high school. But when it came time for college, Ray decided to attend Columbus State Community

College while Samuel went off to the University of Pennsylvania. The way Samuel saw it, getting into and graduating from an Ivy League school was the ultimate con. Unfortunately, it was one con that Ray had to sit out.

Ray wiped his hands on his shirt. "You fellas have grown a bit since the last time I saw you." Jackson noticed the new gold caps he sported on his front teeth.

"Your dad here?" Jackson asked.

"He's downtown. Some old lady locked herself out of her apartment." He smiled, his gold caps sparkling. "It's a total coincidence that she lives above a jewelry store." Ray sat on a stool. "How's your brother?"

"He just got an A on his last exam."

"Whose paper did he cheat off?"

Jackson laughed. "He says you should call him."

"He's the busy one, not me. Every time I call he's off to some toga party."

Jackson doubted his brother would attend any toga parties — not unless he was trying to steal a sorority girl or two — but he didn't want to waste any more time talking about Samuel. "I need a favor."

Ray whistled as Jackson unfolded the schematic plans on the counter. "Is that a —"

"Yep."

"Now this . . . *this* is a key," Ray said. "Wait. Are you asking what I think you're asking?"

"According to our tech guy, the dimensions of the grooves are within 1/64 of an inch tolerance."

Ray tapped the plans. "I know I'm not a college boy

like your brother, but unless I'm mistaken, Guttenbabel keys aren't supposed to be duplicated."

Charlie pulled two fifty-dollar bills from his pocket and placed them on the counter. "Ulysses S. Grant says otherwise," he said, sliding the money across the glass, leaving a trail in the dust. "Can you get us a copy by Wednesday afternoon?"

Eyeing the money, Ray said, "While I enjoy General Grant's company, there's no way I can get this done by Wednesday. Guttenbabels have both mechanical and electrical components. It's got to be the right blend of copper, silver, and aluminum alloy, or the key won't carry the current necessary to trigger the lock. And because of the strength of the metal, the key can't be cut like a regular key — it has to be punched." He spun the bills. "It'll take five days to get the metal, and three days after that to finish the key."

"That's an eight-day turnaround. Samuel said you could do it in five." Jackson placed two additional bills on the counter. "My friend Ben Franklin says the same."

X'S AND O'S

Although Keith Sinclair kept his gaze glued to his tuna sandwich, his abundant interest in his lunch had nothing to do with the quality of the meal. Rather, it was his futile attempt to ignore all the posters plastered around the cafeteria, half of which featured his face crossed out with a big, red X. The two sixth graders sitting at his table, usually eager to talk to Keith about basketball or video games or whatever else he wanted to discuss, ate their lunches and slinked off without saying a word.

"About time they left," Stewart Hogan said, dropping into the chair across from Keith. "We need to talk."

Keith sighed. He'd pick those sixth graders over Stewart any day. "I heard Megan broke things off with you."

Stewart nodded. "Tell me the truth. Did you tell her that you gave me the game? You know how she feels about you."

"Believe me, the feeling is mutual," Keith said. "But I didn't tell her. Maybe she just got tired of all your bragging."

"It wasn't bragging. I just needed a little more time." He banged the table. "She came over on Saturday. I almost kissed her. I was *this* close."

"Of course you were," Keith said, his voice as dry as the tuna. "Now why are you sitting here again? Our agreement was never based on you actually taking her to the formal."

"I know. I just had to ask. I don't know how else she could have found out about the game. Seriously, I didn't tell anybody."

"Neither did I."

Stewart rose. "You'll understand if I keep the game."

Keith had already gone back to his sandwich. "No problem. I own two copies."

"And don't worry about me and the formal. I'll find another girl to take. I mean, I'm Stewart Hogan."

Keith rolled his eyes. *And people say I'm arrogant.*

As soon as Stewart left the table, Wilton slid into the chair beside Keith. "Was he bragging again?"

"Of course. But forget about him. What did you find out?"

"I talked with Mr. Pritchard. He's going to make Carmen remove all the posters with your face. They won't be allowed to run that ad about you in the newspaper. And he won't let the Art Geeks erect that sculpture of you as a wolf." Wilton let out a long stream of air. "But there's nothing he can do about SAKS. Any organization is allowed to campaign on behalf of a candidate."

"Maybe I should talk to Carmen," Keith said. "*Persuade* her to change her mind."

"Or maybe you should just let it go," Wilton said. "With Kelsey on your side, there's no way Gaby can win."

Keith took another bite of his sandwich. Half of the tuna dropped from the bread onto his tray, but he didn't notice. He wouldn't admit it to Wilton, but Keith still didn't know exactly how Dr. Kelsey planned to fix the election. Every time Keith met with him, the only thing the man seemed interested in was the money that Keith's father had promised "the school."

"Carmen's smart, but there's no way she came up with this on her own," Keith said. "Someone helped her."

"Jackson?"

"Who else? For all I know, Jackson's the one who tipped Megan off. He never knows when to quit."

"But who cares? You're going to win."

"Oh, I'll win all right. I'll crush Gaby. And Jackson." Keith nodded across the cafeteria toward Charlie de la Cruz, who was talking to some kid with paint splattered across his T-shirt. "Talk to Tommy and Trevor. For the next few days, I want to keep an eye on Jackson and Charlie. If anyone even looks in their direction, I want to know who they are." He finished his sandwich. "Jackson Greene doesn't know who he's messing with."

Jackson Greene wasn't just on Keith Sinclair's mind. On the other side of the cafeteria, while Lynne described her dress for the formal — and pointed out that Gaby had yet to pick one — Gaby found herself staring at the walls, taking in all the posters. Even though Mr. Pritchard was making SAKS scale back their campaign, the damage had been done — Omar's latest poll showed Gaby capturing a third of the jock vote and half of the sixth-grade vote. She had felt self-conscious about all the attention at first, but as student after student stopped her in the hallways and in class, telling her that they planned to vote for her, she began to believe that (1) she just might become Maplewood's next Student Council president, and (2) a lot of it was due to Jackson Greene.

She wasn't sure which of those facts scared her more.

Lynne cleared her throat. "You haven't heard a word I've said, have you?"

"Sorry, I'm just . . . Sorry." She took a bite of her sandwich, frowned, then dropped her food on her tray. "You finished? Want to go to the library?"

Lynne nodded. "So you want to tell me what you're thinking about so hard?" she asked after they turned in their trays. "And don't say you're thinking about Omar. He walked by our table three times, and you barely looked in his direction."

Gaby looped her thumbs in her pockets. "You know this is all because of Jackson, right? Carmen's campaign was his idea."

"It sounds like something he'd think of. You know a boy really has to like you to go through all this trouble to get you elected."

Gaby tugged on her ponytail. "I'm supposed to be mad

at him. He kissed another girl. I thought he felt . . ." She shook her head and tried again. "I'm going to the formal with Omar."

"They both really like you," Lynne said. "And Omar's . . . nice. But even I have to admit he's no Jackson Greene. Maybe you should break up with him."

"Break up? We're not together."

"You know what I mean."

Gaby nodded. "I know. It's not fair to Omar. I just . . . I just wish I knew how Jackson felt."

"Has he shown any interest in anyone since Katie?"

"According to Charlie, he doesn't talk to any girls."

"Except you." Lynne opened the library door. "Maybe you should just . . . I don't know . . . tell him how you feel. It's a little crazy how you can plan to give a speech in front of the entire school with no problem, but you can't tell one boy how you might feel about him."

"But I'm supposed to be —"

"I know, I know," Lynne said. "But haven't you ever heard of a cease-fire?"

THE **INSIDE MAN** (LITERALLY)

After a quick afternoon snack, Jackson changed clothes, trading in his tie and blazer for jeans and a T-shirt. He was heading to the Shimmering Hills Library to meet Charlie. They were working on a project and wouldn't be finished until 8:00 p.m. or so.

At least, that's what he told his father that morning.

Jackson was about to walk out the door when a message popped onto his laptop screen.

IAmBorgHearMeRoar: Can I come?

IAmBorgHearMeRoar: Jackson?

IAmBorgHearMeRoar: I know you're there. Your bike's in the driveway.

IAmBorgHearMeRoar: Please???!!!

OptimusGreene: We shouldn't be talking like this. Meet me outside.

Jackson found Hashemi standing by his bike. Hashemi wore black cargo pants and a black turtleneck, and he held a black ski mask.

"My gloves are in my backpack," Hashemi said. "I couldn't find any black ones, so I spray-painted Mom's yellow kitchen gloves. Is that all right?"

Jackson looked him up and down. "Did you bring a pair of pliers?"

A look of horror crossed Hashemi's face. "I knew I forgot something —"

"Hash, really, it's okay."

It was only then that Hashemi noticed Jackson's clothes. "Wait? I thought we were —"

"We are."

"But I thought this is what people wore when they —"

"It is. In the movies. When it's dark outside." Jackson glanced in the direction of the sun, which barely touched the tree line. "I know you think this is exciting, but are you sure you want to do this? It could be risky."

"Risk is my middle name," Hashemi said. "Well, it's actually Ferydoon, but you get —"

"Hashemi. There's nothing wrong with being the tech guy. You're good at it. You're a key part of the team."

"But in the movies, the tech guy is always an uber-nerd." Jackson crossed his arms.

"Okay, yes, I'm a nerd. But I'm not an uber-nerd. I'm a cool nerd. I'm the type of nerd that —"

"That breaks into a school to scope out office equipment?"

"I was going to say 'that takes risks,' but that works too."

"Do you at least have your cell phone?"

Hashemi pulled and tugged and pulled some more, and finally extracted the MAPE from his pocket. "What do you need me to do? I upgraded the GPS chips — they're so precise, I can pinpoint our location within a six-inch radius. I can also —"

"Can you text on it yet?"

"For the most part. Just avoid *G*, *H*, and *J* and you'll be okay." Hashemi's face fell. "Unfortunately, the dialing features are cutting into the phone's stand-by time. Now it only lasts for five days on a charge."

Jackson patted Hashemi's shoulder. "What's life without a few risks?"

Charlie sat curled into a ball in the corner of the school's smallest janitorial closet, surrounded by mops, brooms, and plungers that had seen far better days. According to Jackson, the janitorial service wasn't scheduled to clean the bathrooms until later that night, so they had plenty of time. Of course, that was easy for Jackson to say, as he wasn't the one crammed into a dark, contained space with hazardous materials.

Finally, Charlie's cell phone buzzed.

We're ere.

Charlie stretched his legs as he stepped out of the closet and into the silent school. It was surreal, being in a place so quiet. At his house, the television was always blaring, or people were always talking. He wondered if this was how it felt at Jackson's house now that Samuel was gone. It had to be great, having so much free time to yourself. Jackson didn't have to worry about sharing the TV or finding a quiet place to use the phone. He wasn't the low man on the totem pole, taking orders from his mom and his dad and his sister.

Jackson Greene was the luckiest boy he knew.

Charlie entered Mrs. Cooper's room — the lock hadn't worked in years — and cracked open the window. " 'We're 'ere'?" he asked Jackson.

He shrugged. "It's in beta. Now move so we can get in."

Jackson leapt into the room, avoiding the loose pane of glass that rattled when touched, the splintered windowsill that left shards of wood in your palm, and the stacks of books and papers lined up underneath the window. It was as if he had done this hundreds of times before.

Hashemi eventually made it into the room, his hands red and raw, his breaths short and shallow, and his ankle gimpy from landing on an ancient copy of *Webster's Dictionary*.

Once they reached the main office, Jackson slipped the bump key into the lock. Two taps later, the door creaked open.

"That was easy," Hashemi whispered.

"This ain't my first rodeo, cowboy. But this isn't the door I'm worried about." Jackson pulled the newly punched copy room key from his pocket. The edges were almost too sharp to touch.

They made their way through the office, which was just as dark and silent as the rest of the school. At the door to the copy room, Jackson offered up a silent prayer and shimmied the key into the lock. It caught halfway, and the boys gasped. Jackson jiggled the key and applied a bit more pressure, and after a few seconds that seemed to stretch into hours, the key slid securely into the lock.

It was only after the door popped open that Jackson realized he had been holding his breath.

While Hashemi and Charlie examined the Scantron machine, Jackson surveyed the room. Samuel had gotten most of the details correct. It wasn't awe-inspiring. Copiers, printers, and fax machines lined the walls, and a small closet stood at the rear of the room. He opened the closet door to find stacks of boxes and papers, each pile threatening to topple at the slightest touch.

"Charlie," he called. "Got a second?" After Charlie joined him, Jackson asked, "What do you think? Could someone my size fit in here?"

Charlie chewed on his thumbnail. "We'd have to move some of the boxes around, but it should be able to serve as the Fallout Shelter."

"You can't just call it a hiding place, can you?" Jackson took a step back and squinted. "But we may have a problem. With the Scantron machine all the way over on the other side of the room, we need a surefire way to trigger the big reveal. The closet — sorry, the Fallout Shelter — isn't close enough. . . ."

Charlie snapped his fingers. "You know what we need? A Robot in Disguise!"

"That's exactly what I was thinking," Jackson said. "And you've really got to stop watching those Ocean's movies."

"Don't blame me. I didn't invent cable television."

Jackson rattled the closet's lockless handle. Then he glanced at Hashemi. "How's it coming with the Scantron machine?"

"It's not a Scantron machine. I mean — it scans ballots and tests, but it's not an official Scantron machine. It's a . . ." Hashemi paused as he spun the machine around. "It's a Techno . . . a Technomoso . . ." He gave up. "It's not a Scantron machine."

"Fine. How are you doing with the not-a-Scantron machine?"

Hashemi picked up his screwdriver. "Well, it's nothing like the diagrams I looked at online. Because it's so prehistoric, it'll be a bit of a challenge to rig."

"But you can do it, right?"

For once, Hashemi was able to grin at a frowning Jackson Greene. "Of course. It's even got a USB built into it. I should be able to hack it and control it remotely. When they run the ballots, I can set exactly what the tally will be."

"We're not looking for anything fancy," Charlie said. "We just need it to give a false report."

"Sure," Hashemi said. "But I was thinking, since I've got some time on my hands, maybe I could wire it so I could control anything that passed through it. Tests, ballots, whatever. Since this is so ancient, I'd have to run a C++ algorithm to —"

"Love the ambition, love the drive, but remember the plan," Jackson said.

"But there's nothing wrong with improving —"

"That's what you keep saying about the MAP," Charlie said. "And we all see how that's going."

"MAPE," Hashemi said, his voice rising. "And when I finish, it will be the most advanced, most technologically astute —"

"It's an overdesigned paperweight," Charlie said. "You can't even use *H*!"

"It's in beta!"

"Don't mind Charlie," Jackson said, squeezing Charlie's shoulder. "He always gets cranky when I make him sit in a cramped closet for too long." He eyed the not-a-Scantron machine. "But he's right. It just needs to show that Gaby won."

Hashemi sighed. "But that's so . . . simple."

"Rule Number Eleven: Don't use a battering ram when a crowbar will do."

Hashemi blinked. "I don't even know what a crowbar is."

Charlie walked off toward the closet, mumbling under his breath.

"Got everything you need?" Jackson asked. "I want to place the order first thing tomorrow. Ray knows a guy who can probably get us a good deal on the machine."

Hashemi removed a smudge of ink from his glasses. "Almost done. I need a few more minutes to write down all the processor parts."

"Take your time," Jackson said, looking at the closet. "Charlie and I have some rearranging to do."

GaBY MaKes AN eXecuTIVe DecISION

While Jackson, Charlie, and Hashemi crept around the copy room, moving boxes and recording megabytes, Gaby sat at her desk, working on her campaign speech.

So far, she had succeeded in writing and erasing three lines over the last half-hour.

She gave up and opened her email. Carmen had sent proofs for a new set of posters and flyers. Even though Gaby didn't always agree with SAKS's approach to campaigning, she enjoyed working with them, especially Carmen. The girl was really smart when she was focused. Smart and fearless. Most importantly, she believed in Gaby's message — which is more than Gaby could say for the rest of her campaign committee.

She eyed the phone. She knew this day had been coming for a while, but even now, she hated making the call.

Finally, she dialed Lynne.

"Where were you today?" Gaby asked. "You missed the meeting with Mrs. McCoy about increasing the Botany Club budget."

"I had to buy shoes for the formal," Lynne said, her mouth full. "I figured you could handle it without me."

"Omar was there."

"Of course he was." Lynne finally swallowed whatever she was eating. "He's in love with you."

"He cares about the issues. He cares about —"

"He cares because you care."

Gaby stood and slid the keyboard tray underneath the desk. "Lynne, you know why I'm calling. The speeches are next week, and the election is ten days away." She glanced at the official yearbook photo of the girls' basketball team from last year. "I need someone as dedicated as I am."

Lynne was quiet for a few seconds, then said, "So are you firing me?"

Gaby dropped to the edge of her bed. "You're so busy with your brothers and school and everything, I think the campaign committee would totally understand that you need to resign." Even now, she wanted to help Lynne find an honorable way out. Maybe she *was* too nice.

"Yeah," Lynne said, her voice getting stronger. "That makes sense."

Gaby loosened her hair. "You could have been a great campaign manager, you know."

She sighed. "I wish. But it just isn't in me. I'm not like you. You care so much about . . . well, about everybody. That's why you'll make a great president."

Gaby smiled. "You'll still be on my campaign committee, right?"

"Of course. I'll even take directions from old Stick-in-the-Mud."

"I'm not so sure Omar would be the best campaign manager either. He's a little too eager to please."

"Like I said, he's kinda-sorta in love with you."

Gaby fell backward on the bed. "I need someone who's willing to argue with me. I don't want to be like Keith, surrounded by people who bow at his feet." She twisted her hair around her finger. "I'm thinking about asking Carmen. Now that she's toned down her message, there's no reason that we shouldn't be officially working together."

Lynne tsked. "That won't go over so well with Omar."

"Yeah, but I bet that'll be the least of Omar's worries." She grabbed a pillow and pulled it to her chest. "Now tell me about those shoes. Actually, tell me about all your plans for the formal."

JaCKSON aND THE **COOKIE** JaR

The next morning, Jackson entered the kitchen to find his father at the table, a coffee cup in his hand and a couple of chocolate chip cookies on an otherwise empty plate.

"When does Mom get back again?" Jackson asked as he pulled a bowl from the cabinet.

"Why? You complaining about my cooking?"

"Of course not," Jackson said, trying to keep the laughter out of his voice. "I love eating toast and Bran Flakes in the morning."

"Nothing wrong with being regular, son."

After Jackson fixed his cereal, his father cleared his throat. "I called the library." Even though his voice was serious, a hint of a smile crept onto his face. "It's closed on Wednesdays. Budget cuts."

Jackson tapped his spoon on the edge of the bowl. "Internet research," he mumbled. "It ain't what it used to be."

"As Dad used to say, 'Secondhand research yields D-minus results.'"

"I know, I know — Rule Number Twelve."

"Don't let your mother hear you saying that. I'm still catching flack for letting you and Samuel spend so much time with your granddad." He bit into a cookie. "How was I supposed to know he was turning you two into junior criminal masterminds?"

"He taught you the same things."

"Yes, but I use my powers for good, not evil." Donald Greene sipped his coffee. "You know your mom will be devastated if you get into trouble again."

"But I'm not —"

"Don't forget who you're talking to. I was you before you were even born."

Jackson looked at his father. "So now what?"

"You're old enough to know right and wrong, and to deal with the consequences of your actions." He picked up his last cookie. "Whatever you have cooked up, I hope it's worth it."

Jackson shoveled a spoonful of cereal into his mouth and said, "It has to do with Gaby."

His father laughed so hard that tears formed in the corners of his eyes. "I wish your granddad were here — I'd love to see the look on his face. Here you are, barely thirteen, and you're already breaking the Code of Conduct."

"What? I'm not —"

"Rule Number Three: Never con for love."

Jackson coughed, spraying milk and cereal all over the table. He tried to swallow the remaining cereal in his mouth. "Dad, I'm not . . . It isn't like that. . . . I don't —"

"Love. Like. It's all the same."

Jackson grabbed a handful of napkins and began sopping up the milk. "Didn't you steal Mom from that guy she was dating in college by orchestrating a fight between her boyfriend and the swim team?"

"Allegedly."

"Dad . . ."

"What can I say? Some rules are made to be broken." He rose from the table. "And it was the equestrian team."

Jackson watched his father put his mug in the sink. "That's it?" he asked.

"That's it," he said. "The rest is up to you."

Jackson looked at his cereal, now more soggy than crisp. "You mind handing me that cookie?"

His father frowned as he shoved the cookie into his own mouth. "Now what type of parent would I be if I allowed my kid to eat cookies for breakfast?"

THE TRUTH WILL SET YOU FREE

Gaby walked into the living room, her cell phone in her hand. The aroma of chicken and onions hung in the air — her mother was cooking *arroz con pollo* for dinner — but she was too nervous to worry about food. Her mother looked respectable in a white blouse and jeans. Her father, on the other hand, sported a T-shirt that struggled to stretch across his belly and a pair of sweatpants covered in green, brown, and black paint splotches. At least she didn't have to worry about Charlie. He was out doing who knows what with Jackson.

"I just talked to Omar," she said. "He'll be over in ten minutes."

Her father didn't turn away from the TV. "Okay."

"You're changing, right?"

"What? In the middle of the sixth inning? The Indians are up."

"Daddy . . ."

He sniffed his armpit. "Not too ripe. As long as the kid doesn't try to hug me, I should be fine."

"Daddy!"

"When did it become illegal for a man to wear what he wanted to wear inside his own house?"

Gaby planted her hands on her hips. "Mom, will you make Dad change?"

Elena de la Cruz glanced up from her paperback. "Hector, why must you torment your daughter so?"

"'Cause it's fun." He flipped to another channel — a football game. Ohio State was throttling a team Gaby didn't recognize. "You and Omar shooting hoops again? Remind him that he's supposed to get the ball *through* the rim."

"Daddy!"

"I'm glad you're getting a chance to meet this boy, Elena," her father said, rising from his seat. "He's . . . nice. . . . Though, as my *abuelo* would say, that boy is *mas lento que una caravana de cobos*."

"A caravan of crabs? He's not *that* slow."

"You'd think he'd be black and blue, as many times as you 'fouled' him the other day. And I could tell you were holding back. Trying not to show him up." He tugged his daughter's ponytail. "That's why I like it when you play with Jackson. Neither one of you backs down."

Gaby's mother closed her paperback. "Jackson was here? I didn't realize you two had made up."

"We haven't."

Her father grunted. "Could have fooled me, the way you two were playing and laughing."

"We weren't laughing. And I can't believe you were spying on me!"

"When did it become illegal for a man to watch his —"

"Daddy!"

"Fine, I'm going." He stood up and kissed Gaby's cheek. "I want to look my best for this nice guy who doesn't know how to dribble a ball."

Gaby collapsed on the couch after he left the room. "He's impossible!"

"He's just giving you a hard time." Her mother picked up the remote and muted the television. "So Jackson was over here the other day? Did you have fun?"

Gaby nodded. "I forgot how much I liked playing with him."

"But not Omar?"

"I'm not one of your patients, Mom. Stop trying to get into my head."

"Honey, I'm only trying to be your mother. Nothing more. But I have to be honest — the formal is in a week, and you haven't asked me once to take you shopping for a new dress. This is your first real date, and you're acting like it's not a big deal."

"It's just some stupid dance."

"Then why was it so important last year? You dragged me to three different malls, remember?" She stared at her daughter. "Was it because you went as a big group last year? Or was it because a certain boy was part of that group?"

"Mom . . ."

"Okay, okay." She patted her daughter's knee. "So why is Omar coming over? Are you two playing basketball again?"

"Yeah, for a while. Then . . . Then I have to tell him something." She picked up a pillow from the couch and fluffed it. "I'm going to ask Carmen to be my campaign manager."

Gaby's mom nodded. "From what you say about Carmen, she'll be a great manager."

"That's not all." Gaby focused on the pillow in her lap. "I'm going to tell Omar that I don't like him. I mean, I like him, but as a friend. We can still go to the formal together, but as a group, with Lynne and Fiona and everyone else."

"That's probably smart. It was pretty obvious that you didn't truly like him."

"Really?"

She smiled. "It doesn't take a psychology degree to figure out who you actually like."

Gaby exhaled as she loosened her ponytail. "He kissed another girl, Mom."

"Well, yes. But as I understand it, it was just a slight —"

"Mom!" She swung the pillow at her mother's legs. "Are you seriously taking Jackson's side in this?"

"I'm not taking his side, *mija*. It's just . . . Jackson's mother and I had lunch last month. I think he's really sorry for what he did. And even though he's one of the smartest kids I've ever met, he's still just a boy. And boys — especially thirteen-year-old boys — can be as dense as a box of rocks . . . especially when it comes to girls they like."

Gaby raked her hair over her face, creating a dark, shiny curtain. "What should I do?"

"You're a smart girl, Gabriela." Her mother grabbed the remote and turned the television volume up. "I'm sure you'll figure it out."

They sat like that for a while — Gaby with her hair in her face, and Gaby's mother watching a game she had no interest in — until the doorbell rang.

Gaby pulled her hair back into a ponytail and went to the door.

"Hello," Omar said. "I mean, *hola*."

Gaby's mother rose and introduced herself. "I've heard so many . . . nice things about you. What brings you over?"

"Gaby suggested that I come over so we could shoot some hoops. She missed quite a few threes the other day, so I thought I could give her some pointers. Then I thought we could maybe work on her campaign." He looked sideways at Gaby. "That is, of course, if that's what you want to do."

"Oh, I see," Gaby's mother said, her eyes on her daughter.

"Plus, I figured Gaby and I could talk about colors for the formal. I ordered a tux, but —"

"You ordered a tux?" Gaby reeled backward. "You know this isn't prom, right? It's just a dance."

Elena de la Cruz placed her hand on her daughter's shoulder and gave it a small squeeze. "I'll be in the kitchen."

Gaby looked into Omar's eyes. He was nice. So nice. Too nice for what she was about to do. "Let's shoot some hoops." She opened the door. "And then, after, let's talk. About everything."

KEITH EVENS THE ODDS

As Gabriela de la Cruz stood in her driveway, showing a nice — but mediocre — basketball player how to *really* play, Keith Sinclair sat in the Whetstone branch of the Columbus Metropolitan Library System (which, unlike the Shimmering Hills Library, was open seven days a week). As much as it pained him to admit it, Keith knew he wasn't as smart as Jackson Greene. But as Keith saw it, with all the money, strength, and soon-to-be power he possessed, he didn't need to be overly crafty.

Keith reached for his cell phone as it vibrated on the table.

> I'm here.

Keith texted his location, then sat up and smoothed the wrinkles from his shirt. Although the boy walking into the library didn't know it yet, he was about to get the offer of a lifetime.

All he had to do was sell out Jackson Greene.

CODE BLUE

With fewer than five days before the election, things seemed to be going extremely well for Jackson and his crew — or, as Bradley secretly called them, Gang Greene.

It had taken all weekend, but they had bubbled in ballots for all 371 Maplewood students (they had Gaby winning by a believable but respectable margin). And though Jackson had yet to see the proof, Hashemi claimed he was almost finished with the modifications to the not-a-Scantron machine. Even Victor, usually a wellspring of complaints and gripes, had offered to pay for a celebratory dinner for the group after the election.

Things were going so smoothly, Jackson gave the team Monday afternoon off. Hashemi decided to take a much-needed trip to the electronics store to pick up coding books for the universal translator he was building for the Tech Club. Sure, he was slightly behind schedule — the program was still in beta — but he was confident that with a few tweaks, it would be the most advanced translation program ever created.

When he returned to the shed, he paused upon notic-
ing the open door. The padlock was lying on the ground.
He glanced at his watch. He was sure that Jackson was
still at school — the Botany Club was in the middle of fall
pruning — and no one else had a key to the shed.

He pushed the door open, then dropped his bag of
manuals.

The worktable containing the schematics, the ballots, and the machine was bare — except for a small,
folded note.

Hashemi read the note, then whipped his head toward
the pegboard where all the keys for the job resided.

Empty.

Hashemi fished through his book bag, finally getting
his fingers around the MAPE. He punched the only number he had ever dialed into the phone.

"Charlie, we've got a Code Blue."

Jackson arrived at the shed to find the door still gaping
open. Charlie, Hashemi, and Bradley huddled around the
worktable in the middle of the room.

"It's gone," Charlie said as Jackson entered. "It's all gone."

Jackson's gaze bounced around the room. "Everything?"

"Well, not my action figures," Hashemi said. "But
everything for the election job is gone." While he hated
being ransacked, he was thankful that the thief had left
his memorabilia unharmed.

"So now what?" Bradley asked.

"So now we get ready to kiss up to President Keith Sinclair," Hashemi said. "Without the keys, we can't get into the main office and the copy room. Without the not-a-Scantron, we can't switch out the machine. Without the ballots, we can't ask for a recount." Hashemi plopped onto a stool. "It's over."

Jackson patted Hashemi's shoulder. "Don't be so down. As my grandfather used to say, 'Diamonds are created under extreme pressure.'"

"So are explosions," Hashemi mumbled.

"Remind me to teach you how to respond to a pep talk." Jackson turned to Charlie. "Anyone heard from Victor?"

Charlie shook his head. "We've been trying to contact him all afternoon."

Bradley took in a gulp of air. "Do you think Victor sold us out?"

"Maybe. If the offer was good enough." Jackson popped his knuckles. "It had to be Keith."

"Whoever it was, you'll find out soon enough," Hashemi said as he handed him the note he had found on the table. "You're supposed to meet him in an hour."

Keith sat at a picnic table at Fitzgerald Park, surrounded by kids playing on the swings and jungle gym. From his seat, he could hear the cheers from the basketball court on the other side of the park — the very court where he had lost to Jackson four months ago.

Funny how things change, Keith thought as Jackson marched toward the picnic table. Although Jackson sported his usual tie and blazer, his trademark grin was absent from his face.

"Surprised?" Keith asked after Jackson sat down.

"No. It had to be you." Jackson brushed a stray leaf from the wooden table. "What did you offer Victor?"

"I promised him that I wouldn't cut the Chess Team's budget."

"And do you plan to keep that promise?"

Keith shrugged. "Depends on how much the Gamer Club's new AV equipment costs."

Jackson tugged at his collar, loosening his red tie. "What do you want?"

Even though Keith had a specific reason for calling Jackson here — a worthy, perhaps even honorable reason — he couldn't help but blurt out: "I wanted you to know who beat you."

"You haven't won yet."

"I have your Scantron machine —"

"It's not a Scantron machine."

"Whatever. I have the machine, the ballots you guys spent so much time filling out, and the keys to every room and file cabinet you need to crack. Even if you could replace all those things in time — which I know you can't — you don't have the money to do it." Keith grinned. "Admit it. You're beat."

Jackson rose from the table. "If you just wanted to gloat, you're wasting my time."

"Wait. Maybe I do have something to offer." Keith

watched as Jackson sank back into his seat. "I think it's time to call a truce."

"Yeah, right."

"I'm serious." Keith forced himself to meet Jackson's gaze. "If I wanted to be mean, I could have taken all of Hashemi's silly dolls —"

"Action figures."

"Call them whatever you want. I could have taken them and everything else in that shed. But I didn't. I *chose* not to. I didn't want to escalate things like you always do."

"You know the rules," Jackson said. "Hashemi's stuff is off-limits. If you had actually taken it . . ."

"Not everyone lives by your silly Code of Conduct," Keith reminded Jackson. "But I did, this one time, because I'm tired of fighting. So here's the deal. If you promise not to retaliate — if you let me be Student Council president and promise not to show me up at any other events — I'll give the Botany Club enough money for seed and fertilizer and whatever other crap you need."

Jackson studied Keith. "How do I know you'll keep your word?"

"You don't. But I respect you, Jackson. You're smarter than you look. And quite frankly, I'm tired of dealing with you." Keith paused as a roar escaped from the basketball courts. "If I can buy your cooperation with the Botany Club, so be it."

"What about the other clubs?"

"Why do you care?" Keith asked. "You're getting what you want. Isn't that enough?"

Jackson remained quiet for a few minutes. He may have been a master planner, but he hadn't counted on this. It was actually quite smart of Keith — if he was telling the truth.

Another roar came from the basketball courts. Jackson still remembered how he felt when he passed Gaby the ball for the last shot of the Blitz. He had trusted her, and she had delivered.

"Good luck with the election," Jackson said, rising from his seat. "You'll need it."

"You know you can't win."

"Maybe I don't have to. From the way it sounds, plenty of people are lining up to vote for Gaby," he said. "Have you thought about what would happen if you lost the election? If Gaby beat you? Talk about embarrassing."

Keith crossed his arms. "That's not going to happen."

Jackson pulled his tie back into place. "Like I said before — good luck."

a NEW PLan

Two hours later, Jackson stood in front of Charlie, Hashemi, and Bradley. His Earl Grey tea, long cold, sat abandoned on the worktable.

Hashemi slammed his fist on the table. "The next time I see Victor —"

"You're not going to do anything," Jackson said. "We don't work like that."

"But he —"

"Victor isn't the problem here. We have four days, no money, no machine, no keys. Nothing." Jackson looked every one of them in the eye. "But I have a plan. It's risky. And if we get caught —"

"I'm in," Charlie said.

"Me too," Hashemi said. "Nerds aren't supposed to sell out other nerds. It's in the handbook."

Jackson turned to Bradley. "What about you?"

"If it wasn't for you guys, I would have spent the last three weeks at home by myself. So yeah, I'm in."

Jackson nodded at the group. "Hash, if I got a new machine by Wednesday afternoon, what could you do with it?"

"I couldn't rig it like I did the old one." Hashemi looked at a schematic on his laptop, which he luckily had with him at the time of the shed robbery. "I had to rebuild the motherboard on the other one. There's no way that I can do that in two days."

"I don't need you to totally reprogram the machine," Jackson said. "I just need you to break it."

"Sure," Hashemi said. "Breaking is easy."

"We're also going to need communication equipment," Jackson said. "Something that allows us all to talk to each other and that's easy to hide. Can you handle that, too?"

"By Friday?" Hashemi opened a new browser on the laptop. "The hardware won't be a problem, but setting up the right software might be a little tricky. Maybe I can use some of the programming from the universal translator."

Jackson moved his cup of tea and picked up the MAPE, which had been serving as a coaster. "Bradley, see if you can get me a copy of the main office key so I can create another bump key. I'll take care of getting a new machine."

"Where will we get the money?" Bradley asked.

"Let me worry about that," Jackson said. He walked away from the group, with Charlie a few steps behind him.

"What?" Jackson asked. "I know you're worried about money, but I can tap into my savings —"

"Forget about the money for a second," Charlie said. "We need an Eckersley."

"A closer? For who?"

"Who do you think?" Charlie looked over his shoulder. "Hash is in over his head. That's a lot of work for him to do by the end of the week."

Jackson leaned against the wall. "Megan?"

"She could help out during the actual heist as well. She'd be a much better White Rabbit than me or Bradley. And the word is she got a big birthday check from her grandmother last month. Given the right motivation, I bet she'd be happy to spend it."

Jackson glanced at Hashemi, his body hunched over his laptop. "I don't know. . . ."

"Come on, Jackson. Stop being a hypocrite. How can you ask Gaby to forgive you when you can't even forgive Megan?"

Jackson groaned. "You love bringing your sister into this, don't you?" He stared at the MAPE, then at Hashemi. "Okay, but she's backup only. Hash gets a chance to pull this off first. And she has to prove she can keep her mouth shut before we bring her onto the team."

Charlie nodded. "Sounds fair."

"And you know Mariano Rivera is a better closer than Eck ever was."

Charlie covered his ears. "Don't ever say that around my dad. He might not let you back into the house."

Jackson laughed. "You mind calling Ray about the machine? I need to talk to Hashemi." He shuffled the MAPE from his left hand to his right. "I just realized there's something else I need him to break."

a LEAP OF FAITH

S. —

Just got a text from Traci. AJ dumped Brandy last night. Right before the formal. She already had her dress and everything. Boo hoo. Cry me a river. That's what she gets.

— A.

Megan read the note once more, then looked around. She was sure it had been slipped into her locker by accident, but there was no telling who it was intended for. Sara McGill had the locker next to hers, and Summer Goldberg was two lockers beyond that.

She placed the note in her back pocket and grabbed her books. This wasn't the only strange message she'd received this month. When she had found a note in her bag saying that Stewart had gotten his copy of *Ultimate Fantasy IV* from Keith Sinclair, she hadn't wanted to believe it. But when she asked Stewart, he couldn't even look at her as he tried to fumble his way through a lie.

Keith Sinclair was a sworn enemy of the Tech Club — not even *UF IV* could change that.

(And she had not been *this* close to kissing Stewart, despite what he and his idiot friends thought.)

She slipped into her desk and read the note again. There was nothing like being the first one with hot gossip to share — especially when it involved someone as cruel as Brandy Atkinson. Brandy was the meanest girl at school, maybe even meaner than Keith. No one would shed a tear for her if AJ had dumped her.

"What are you reading?"

Megan clutched the note to her chest. "Nothing."

Emily, her best friend, smirked. "Doesn't look like nothing," she said as she reached for the note. "Let me see —"

"No! I can't. It's not —"

"Come on, Meg. It must be juicy. You're practically drooling."

Megan shook her head. "It's nothing." She shoved the note into her book bag. "Forget you even saw it."

Megan kept her ears and eyes open, hoping for any clue about AJ and Brandy. While the couple usually ate lunch together, come noon, AJ was nowhere to be seen. Later, as Megan passed her locker, she saw Brandy whispering to her best friend. Brandy's eyes may have been red, but Megan wasn't sure.

Megan was beginning to wonder if she should have said something to Emily. Em and the Drama Club always had the inside scoop. Surely they would know what was going on.

But Megan also knew what had happened the last time she had blabbed about something that didn't concern her. She was still trying to make up for that one.

At the end of the day, just before she reached her locker, she saw AJ and Brandy walking down the hall, hand in hand, blatantly ignoring Dr. Kelsey's PDA rules. She opened her locker to find another note.

> Congratulations. You passed.
> Meet me by the swings at the Fitz at 3:30 p.m.
> if you want the entire story.
> — J.

"I should have known you were behind this," Megan said as she sat down at a picnic table across from Jackson. "You're the only guy I know who sends handwritten notes."

"It wasn't just me," Jackson said. "I had a little help from Charlie and Hash — they found a way to delay AJ during lunch —"

"You dragged Hashemi into this?" She balled her hands into fists.

"It was a test. A leap of faith, as Charlie would call it. By the way, I'm sure Brandy and AJ thank you for not spreading any rumors about them."

"Not cool, Jackson. I've been trying to apologize for months —"

"I know, but —"

"Let me finish!" Megan said. "Every time I tried to apologize, you looked like you'd rather chew glass than talk to me. I can't even look at Gaby without feeling guilty. And now you decide to make fun of me by playing some prank?"

"It wasn't a —"

"You're just as bad as Keith!" she yelled. "No, you're worse. You're a . . . a . . . a *DenIb Qatlh*!"

"But I — wait. What did you call me?"

"A Denebian slime devil," Megan said. "In Klingon."

"Didn't know the school offered that language elective," Jackson mumbled. "Look, I'm sorry, but I had to know that I could trust you. And now I do." He placed his notebook on the table. "Don't you want to know why Keith gave Stewart the game? Why Stewart dropped out of the election? How this affects the Tech Club?"

"The Tech Club?" Megan planted her hands on the table. "Tell. Me. Everything."

So he did.

Afterward, he sat there, watching Megan's face become redder and redder as she ranted about Stewart and Keith. Jackson was a bit surprised by the . . . *flavor* of her word choices. He was almost glad that half of her words were in Klingon.

"I wish I could have told you some of this sooner. There's just too much at stake."

"At stake?" She clicked her teeth. "You've got a plan. You want to take Keith down, don't you?"

"Absolutely. Do you want to help?"

"Absolutely."

Jackson scribbled out Hashemi's address and handed it to her. "Meet us here in an hour. Be sure to bring your birthday money."

Hashemi could barely speak. Standing inches away from him was Megan Feldman. Tech Club president. Cheerleader. Goddess.

"So is this why you've been missing Tech Club meetings?" she asked.

"You noticed?"

"Of course," she said. "No one can describe warp core theory like you."

"Um . . ."

Jackson stepped between Hashemi and Megan, then placed his hand under Hashemi's chin and snapped his drooling mouth shut. "Megan, do you know Bradley?" Jackson asked. "You can thank him for delivering all those anonymous messages."

After the introductions, Bradley glanced toward the door, wedged open to let air into the suddenly hot shed. "Are you sure it's safe to meet here?" he asked.

"Keith thinks he has us beat," Charlie replied. "He doesn't have any reason to watch us anymore."

Jackson chuckled. "And, you know, we changed the locks."

"So what's the plan?" Megan asked.

Jackson picked up his cup of tea. "Hashemi. The list."

Hashemi's hand trembled as he handed her the sheet of paper. "As long as we have all these items by tomorrow, I should have enough time to rig everything."

She glanced over the list. "What's a not-a-Scantron machine?" she asked. She looked at Jackson, then at Hashemi. "What are you guys up to?"

Hashemi blinked in reply.

"Charlie, why don't you and Bradley go over the list with Megan, just to make sure we haven't missed anything? I need to talk to Hashemi about the machine."

As Charlie and Bradley led Megan away, Jackson sat on the stool across from Hashemi. "You're acting like you've never spoken to her before."

"I *don't* speak to her. Not in Tech Club meetings. Not anywhere. I just sit and stare."

"But she likes the same types of things you like. You two should have plenty to talk about."

Hashemi removed his glasses and wiped away the sweat that had collected on the frames. "Knowing my luck, she'll fall head over heels for you by the time this is all over."

"She's cute, but she's not my type." Jackson finished his tea. "She doesn't play enough basketball."

THE PEOPLE'S CHOICE

Gaby stood backstage, her speech folded into a tight square in her hands. She didn't need the paper — she had read it enough times to memorize it. It was full of figures and facts and all the information necessary to help her fellow students make an informed decision.

It was also as boring as ketchup flowing out of a bottle.

So while the candidates for historian, then treasurer, then secretary, and then vice president took the stage, Gaby remained as far from the podium as possible, mumbling to herself, walking back and forth along the backstage wall.

Finally, Carmen jumped in front of her. "Keep walking like that and you'll ruin those fancy new shoes of yours."

Gaby looked at her feet. The heels still made her feel off-balance, but they were low enough that she didn't feel like she was about to fall on her face. They were plain navy blue with little silver buckles — nothing like the pair that *Tia* Isabel had forced onto her for the formal last year.

"Don't sweat it," Carmen said. "You know that speech back and forth."

Rule Number Two popped into Gaby's head. *Stay cool under pressure. A rattled crew is a mistake-prone crew.* She was sure that applied to Student Council candidates as well.

Gaby glanced toward the stage when she heard clapping. "Keith's next. I bet he'll say everything I'm going to say."

Carmen snatched the paper from Gaby's hand. "Then say something different."

"Hey, give that back."

Carmen quickly scanned the speech. "Everyone out there's been beaten over the head with facts. At this point, they either believe them or they don't." She handed the paper back to Gaby. "Keith is going to give them a lot of promises about what he's going to do. Remind them of what you've already done."

Gaby looked at the speech. "But if I cut all the facts, my speech won't be long enough."

Carmen laughed. "They just listened to seven other kids babble on. Believe me, shorter is better." She looped her arm around Gaby's. "Come on. It's almost time."

Gaby felt herself leaning on Carmen as they approached the stage. She could see Keith at the podium, his entire body bathed in yellow light. He even held up his thumb like a real politician.

Gaby glanced at the speech once more. Then she handed it to Carmen.

"You sure?" Carmen asked.

Gaby nodded.

Carmen patted her on the shoulder as Keith finished his speech. "Good luck."

Instead of looking out at the crowd, Gaby stared at the podium as she crossed the stage, focusing on the click of her heels against the polished hardwood. She heard one clap, then two, then three, and then, all at once, a sea of applause.

It took a second for her to realize that they were cheering for her.

She reached the podium and adjusted the microphone. She couldn't see into the crowd, but she knew that Omar and Lynne and Fiona and Charlie were in the audience.

She figured Jackson was there as well, cheering just as loud.

"I know you all have been sitting there for a while, so I'll make this short and sweet and to the point."

"Amen," someone called out.

She smiled. "I can recite all the facts and figures about where we are as a school and about where I think we need to go. You've seen these facts — they're on all the fliers I passed out, and they're on all my posters. The facts are clear — Maplewood is a great school with a great student body. But we can be better. And I'm not just talking about improving the athletics or academics. Student Council doesn't exist just for the benefit of the basketball team or the Debate Team. Student Council is here for the entire school.

"I'm sure you've heard other candidates talk about what they plan to do once they're elected. I'm going to talk about what I've already done." She looked down at herself. "Despite the skirt and shoes, you guys know who I am. I'm the same girl now that I was last year, and the year before that. I'm the girl who chased every loose ball in every basketball game I played. I'm the girl who cheers for the football team — no matter the score — and the Chess Team, even if I have to cheer quietly. I'm the girl who proudly served as a Student Council classroom representative last year, which is more than I can say for some of the other candidates." Gaby paused as a few students hooted and hollered. "I am Gabriela de la Cruz. I have always been proud to be a Maplewood Fighting Dolphin. When I'm elected, I will continue to cheer and support you all, both as your friend and your president." She took a step back, then leaned in and yelled, "Go Dolphins!"

They were still cheering when she left the stage.

cease-FIRE

The final bell had rung a few minutes earlier, but Jackson remained at his desk. Even after he closed his notebook and left the classroom, his mind stayed on his notes. The election was only two days away, but his to-do list continued to grow.

Then he rounded the corner, and every item on that list quickly withered away.

It wasn't his locker that made his mind go blank. Rather, it was the girl in the pencil skirt and the navy blue shoes.

"Hey," he said. He quickly took Gaby in — hands behind her back, bangs swept to the left, face blank of emotion. He dropped his book bag (on his foot, but he didn't notice), then went to open his locker.

He paused. It was already unlocked.

Gaby brought her hands from behind her back, revealing the missing padlock. "Just wanted to see if I could still do it."

"Samuel would be proud. He didn't think you were paying attention when he taught us."

"If I'm being totally honest, I didn't pick the lock." She spun the lock around her index finger. "I guessed the combination."

Jackson swallowed what felt like sand. The combination was her birthday.

"That's what I get for being predictable." He caught hold of the padlock and began to pull away, but as soon as her skin brushed against his, he dropped the lock, this time on his other foot.

Gaby stepped back so Jackson could pick up the padlock. She almost tugged her ponytail, but stopped. *If I can talk to an auditorium full of students, I can do this.*

"Charlie's been really giddy over the past few days," she said as Jackson crammed books into his locker. "He's acting like he used to when you two were planning one of your schemes. But you don't do that anymore, right?"

"I heard your speech today," he said. "It was great."

"You didn't answer my question."

"You didn't ask a question. You made a statement, phrased as a question."

"Jackson Greene!" She crossed her arms. "Quit dodging."

"Quit fishing."

"So you're not going to tell me what you guys are up to?"

"Like I said before, I liked your speech. It was very inspiring." He closed his locker. "You're still going to the formal, right?"

She nodded.

"With Omar?"

She hesitated, chewed on the inside of her lip, then nodded. "Yeah. But not as a date. A whole group of us are going together."

Jackson opened his mouth. Closed it. Opened it again. "So you're not going as a couple?"

She shook her head. "No."

Jackson took a deep breath, so long that Gaby thought he was trying to suck all the air out of the hallway, then said, "I wish I had been smart enough to ask you to the formal. I'm sorry. For everything."

They stared at each other — only for a few seconds, but to Gaby, it felt like hours. Days even. She searched his face, looking for the con, the game, the prank, the joke.

All she saw was regret.

"Be sure to tell Omar to buy you a corsage," he said. "Better yet, he should buy you a bouquet." He slung his bag over his shoulder.

"It's not like that with me and Omar. We're just friends." She placed her hand on his arm, squeezing it harder than necessary. "Really. Just friends."

Then, realizing that she was not only touching Jackson Greene but was within kissing distance, Gaby pulled away.

Jackson scratched his jaw. "So if it's not a real date, someone else could bring you a corsage or a bouquet?"

"What? I'm not . . . I mean —"

"I'm speaking hypothetically, of course." He flashed her a smile, and Gaby could feel her heartbeat go super-sonic. "But that doesn't change the fact that you deserve flowers."

Gaby didn't know whether to laugh or hit him. They had avoided each other for four months. She couldn't go from hating him to *this*. Whatever *this* was.

"Why do you care? You're not even going to the formal."

"Are you kidding? I wouldn't miss it."

She blinked a few times as she processed his words. "But I thought you hated dances?"

"I do. But it's worth going, just to see you win."

Gaby watched him back away. His tie, like usual, was slightly to the left. His grin, like always, was wide and rascally.

It wasn't until he had disappeared around the corner that she realized Jackson had misspoken. They would know the election results long before the formal. Perhaps even by lunch.

There's no way — no reason — that the results wouldn't be announced until the formal, she told herself. *Right?*

POLITICS

While Jackson and Gaby were finishing their conversation, Keith was marching through the atrium, not even bothering to apologize as he bumped into student after student. He entered the main office and headed for Dr. Kelsey's door, but before he could knock, Ms. Appleton said, "He's not there."

"But I have an appointment."

"There's nothing I can do about that." She pointed to a chair. "He'll be back momentarily."

Keith trudged to the row of chairs against the wall. A crowd of students passed by the office, their loud voices reminding him of all the cheers for Gaby's speech. He wasn't sure, but he even thought he had seen Stewart clapping for her. The next time he saw him, Keith was going to ask for his video game back.

Finally, a full fifteen minutes after their appointment, Dr. Kelsey entered the office. Keith jumped to his feet. "We need to talk!"

Dr. Kelsey glanced at his watch. He'd been brushing Keith off all day, but apparently the boy couldn't take a hint. "Come on," he said. "But let's make it quick."

Keith followed Dr. Kelsey into the office and slammed the door shut. "What's your plan, Dr. Kelsey? The election is in two days. I can't lose. I have to get into Winstead. If I don't, my dad . . ." He dropped into the chair across from Kelsey's desk. "Is there anything I can do to help?"

"I've got it under control."

"But how —"

"Keith, calm down." Dr. Kelsey could hardly believe this was Roderick Sinclair's son. But maybe this was an opportunity in disguise. He slid open a drawer and pulled out the form that Keith had handed to him a few weeks ago.

"If you really want to help, you can talk to your father about his donation. While it's a generous sum, it's not quite enough to cover all of the school's needs. Perhaps if he increased it by another ten percent. . . ."

Keith squirmed in his seat. "I don't know. Dad's out of town and won't be back until Friday night. I don't think he'd agree to a new deal without discussing it with you first."

"I understand," he said. "Well, I'm sure you'll have more than enough support from the basketball players. They're all voting for you, right?"

Keith narrowed his eyes. "That's not fair."

"That's politics," Dr. Kelsey replied. "And instead of waiting until next week, I'd really prefer that check by tomorrow afternoon. I want to do some shopping this weekend."

Keith glared at Dr. Kelsey for a few seconds, then rose from his chair. "I'll talk to Dad's secretary. I'll get you your check."

"And I'll get you your election."

Dr. Kelsey leaned back in his chair and grinned as Keith stormed out. Why spend all that money on a fancy espresso machine when he could go to Italy and drink it fresh?

REINFORCEMENTS

With the election less than twenty-four hours away, Gang Greene was knee-deep in last-minute preparations. At the worktable in the middle of the shed, Hashemi fiddled with the guts of a small microphone with one hand while pecking at his laptop with the other. A few feet away, Megan, Charlie, and Bradley practiced their roles for Friday. Jackson knelt by the wooden door he had propped against the wall almost four weeks ago. The Guttenbabel was covered in sawdust, handprints, and grime, and, at present, remained unpickable.

Charlie walked over and peeked over Jackson's shoulder. "How's it going? Having any luck?"

Jackson replaced his pliers with a small Phillips screwdriver. "I'll be ready by tomorrow." He nodded toward Megan and Bradley. "How are they doing?"

"Good. Megan's a pro at this."

"And are you ready?"

Charlie shrugged. "I'm just the floater. Pretty easy to be ready when all I'm doing is walking around."

"Charlie, you know the plan. . . ."

"I know. But there's no way you can run point tomorrow. Kelsey's going to be eyeballing you the entire time."

"I can handle it."

Charlie sighed. He knew he should trust Jackson. He hadn't led him astray. Yet.

"How's Hashemi?" Jackson asked.

"Take a wild guess," Charlie said. "I thought you said he worked better under pressure."

"He does. But I think Megan's making him worse."

"Think he'll be mad once he finds out how much we've kept from him?"

"Yeah." Jackson glanced at Megan and Bradley. "But I'm sure he'll get over it."

"If not, you can always offer him a corsage."

Jackson glared at Charlie, who was practically shaking, he was trying so hard to contain his laughter. "You talked to Gaby?" Jackson asked.

A snort escaped from Charlie's lips. "A bouquet? Really?"

"What? Don't all girls like flowers?"

"And what about Omar?"

Jackson quickly unscrewed the lock mechanism from the door and began cleaning it off. "They're just friends."

"He's a nice guy."

"He's as interesting as drying paint."

"But —"

"I've got dead skin cells with more personality."

The smile disappeared from Charlie's face. "Jackson, she's my sister."

"Charlie, you know how I feel. . . . You know what Gaby means . . ." He glanced at the lock in his hands. "Look, I won't screw up again. I'm really trying to keep my promise to her."

"I'm not sure if Gaby would agree."

Jackson slipped the lock back into the door with a satisfying thud. "I guess we'll find out tomorrow."

Charlie offered a hand to Jackson and helped him up. "You'd better deliver on those flowers."

"Already working on it." Jackson dusted off his jeans. "Okay, let's get this over with."

Jackson walked to the worktable while Charlie headed toward Megan and Bradley. Jackson sat down across from Hashemi. "How's it coming?"

"Great. Wonderful." Hashemi plugged another wire into the small circuit board. "Almost finished. Just making a few last-minute tweaks. Improvements, really."

"Really?"

The microphone crackled to life, drowning the room in static. Hashemi coughed. "Clearly the project is in beta —"

"The election is tomorrow."

"I know. I just need to finish this —"

"What's the problem?" Megan asked as she, Bradley, and Charlie approached. "Need some help?"

"No! Of course not!" Hashemi began flipping closed the notebooks and manuals surrounding him, but Megan was already looking at the diagram on the computer screen.

"Hashemi, this is brilliant." She brought her face closer to the screen. "What does this do?" she asked, pointing to a small drawing of a clear box.

Hashemi gulped. "It's a case. It allows the microphone to be heard underwater."

Bradley raised his hand. "Um, are we going swimming tomorrow?"

"No, we're not," Charlie said.

Hashemi adjusted his glasses. "Well, I just thought, since I was already making modifications —"

"Maybe Megan can give you a hand with some of the electronics," Jackson said.

Megan had already nudged Hashemi to the side and was typing away at the laptop. "I'll focus on the software. You handle the hardware."

"The program compiler is very sensitive —"

"I know," she replied, not looking up. "You should download the new version."

"But that hasn't been released yet."

Megan paused. "I have my ways."

"But that's illegal," Hashemi said.

Charlie chuckled. "And rigging testing equipment isn't?"

Jackson glanced at his watch. "Hashemi, maybe you and Charlie could make a run and pick up the rest of the communications equipment."

"Yeah, before you make more *improvements*." Charlie pulled Hashemi out of his seat. "Can your mom give us a ride?"

Jackson's watch beeped five o'clock. "Actually, I might be able to help out with that. . . ."

As Jackson's voice trailed off, a slender young man walked into the shed, his skin smooth and brown and blemish-free, his blazer perfectly tailored to his shape, the sound of his steps nonexistent against the concrete floor.

He loosened his tie, pulling it to the left. "Need some help?"

Jackson grinned. "Guys, I'd like to introduce my brother — the Extraordinary Samuel Greene."

PASSING THE TORCH

In honor of her oldest son returning home for a surprise visit, Miranda Greene served pot roast, greens, and a homemade sweet potato pie. Jackson couldn't help but wish for his brother to visit more often.

After dinner, Samuel followed Jackson to his room. "Got a few minutes?" he asked, already settling at Jackson's desk.

"So why are you really here? And how did you nab a last-minute flight? Ticket prices had to be sky-high."

"I have a friend who didn't mind lending me some of his frequent-flier miles."

Jackson perched on the corner of his bed. "Lend?"

"Okay, so maybe I borrowed them without him knowing. But that's a story for another day. I'm here to talk about you."

Jackson kicked off his shoes. "Who called — Dad or Ray?"

"Dad," he said. "He said you were up to something. Something big."

"You here to talk me out of it?"

Samuel shook his head. "I'm just here to make sure it's not something you can get arrested for."

"Arrested . . . no." Jackson grabbed his notebook. "But expelled . . . As you like to say, that's another story."

"Sounds like a big risk."

"I'm not going to get caught," Jackson said. "Well, probably not."

"Is it worth it?" Samuel leaned forward, his knee almost touching his brother's. "Is *she* worth it?"

"I'm not doing this for Gaby."

"Sorry, I couldn't hear you over all the lies coming out of your mouth."

"Okay. Fine. I'm not doing this *just* for Gaby," Jackson said. "Originally, I hoped this would help her get over the . . . you know . . . the thing with Katie. . . ."

"The Mid-Day PDA?"

Jackson cleared his throat. "You mean the slight brushing of — oh, never mind. Anyway, this is bigger than me and Gaby. Keith Sinclair could ruin the entire school, and Dr. Kelsey is going to help him do it."

"But you care enough to try to stop them?"

"Yeah. And so do Charlie, Hashemi, Bradley, and Megan. And Gaby."

Samuel scratched the back of his head. "Since when did you get a conscience?"

"When I realized it's no fun to lose your best friend," he said. "No thanks to you. . . ."

"Hey, don't blame me. I just told you how to break into the office and suggested that you take Katie along. I didn't tell you to stick your tongue down her throat."

"It was barely a peck!"

Samuel's eyes crinkled. "Why are you always downplaying that kiss?" he asked. "Most guys would love to claim that they locked lips with a girl like Katie Accord."

Jackson stared at his closed notebook, the cover worn with scratches and scuff marks. "When I kiss a girl for the first time — for real — I want it to be with someone I like. With someone who likes me as much as I like her."

"With someone who knows how to play basketball and pick a lock?"

Jackson nodded.

Samuel grabbed a stress ball from the desk and hurled it at Jackson's chest. "What are you trying to do? Make me cry? Enough with the lovefest. Tell me how I can help."

Jackson opened his notebook and quickly ran through the plan, after which Samuel said, "What if Dr. Kelsey —"

"Bradley will be covering him."

"What if Keith doesn't take the bait?"

"Give me some credit. This is Keith Sinclair we're talking about."

"But have you thought of —"

"Enough with the questions." Jackson flipped his notebook shut. "This is my crew. My job."

"I'm just trying to help."

"No, you're trying to take over. I don't need another planner."

"You can't run point tomorrow. Kelsey will be all over you."

"Already got it covered," Jackson said. "What I really

need tomorrow is a driver." He walked to his closet. "And a suit. Something with a lot of pockets."

"I've got just the thing. Be right back."

When Samuel returned, he carried a black garment bag over his arm. "This is the suit I wore to my last Maplewood formal. Given how much you've grown, it should fit. I'll get it cleaned tomorrow." He unzipped the bag and pulled out the suit. "Rule Number Fifteen: If you're going to pull a con, know how to pull a con in style."

SPECIAL DELIVERY

Mrs. Goldman squinted at the young deliveryman carrying the new scoring machine in his wiry, tattooed arms. His face was mostly obscured by a baseball cap pulled low onto his head and large, reflective sunglasses. A thick, scruffy beard covered his cheeks and chin.

She looked at the invoice. "I didn't know we ordered a new machine."

"The district must have ordered it," Ms. Appleton said. "They're always sending us equipment we don't request. Just another example of the school board wasting taxpayer dollars."

The deliveryman cleared his throat. "Ees there anywhere I can put thees?" he asked, his Eastern European accent heavy and thick. "Thees machine ees very, very awkward to hold."

Mrs. Goldman squinted at him again. "Follow me."

The delivery man seemed to hesitate as he entered the copy room, his gaze lingering on the door handle, the metal sparkling underneath the fluorescent lighting.

"You can place it here," she said, tapping the table.

He dropped the new machine on the table, then powered down the old one. "Because eet's a lease, I'm required to take thees one back."

"I'm sorry, but I have to ask — did you ever attend this school?" Mrs. Goldman peered into the deliveryman's face, seeing nothing but her own reflection in his sunglasses. "I feel like I've seen you somewhere before."

The man smiled, showing off a pair of gold-capped teeth. "You must have me mistakeen for someone eelse."

While the deliveryman exited the building, students sat in their homerooms, bubbling in ballots. Jackson stared at his ballot, clean and unmarked, then quickly slipped it into his pocket.

After his homeroom teacher finished passing out the ballots, he raised his hand. "I need a ballot."

Mrs. Lansdale frowned. "But didn't I —"

"You must have skipped me."

She placed another ballot on his desk and watched as he filled it in, line by line.

He pressed down extra hard when bubbling in the circle for Gaby. You could never be too sure when it came to scoring ballots.

Dr. Kelsey had spent the majority of the week thinking about how he was going to confirm Keith's win, but after wasting a few hours bubbling in replacement ballots, he decided to just create a doctored scoring machine report. It would be easy enough to switch it with the real report and shred the ballots. He was the principal, after all. Who was going to challenge him? The Honor Board? The way he saw it, they should just be happy he was letting them participate.

It had taken a lot of discussion — including three pleas from Lincoln — but Dr. Kelsey and the Honor Board had finally come to an agreement concerning the tallying of the votes. The office staff would collect the ballots after homeroom. During lunch, one Honor Board member would be allowed to feed the ballots through the machine. As soon as the scoring was completed, the student was to immediately call for Dr. Kelsey. He would handle printing out the report himself, and that was when he would make the switch.

Dr. Kelsey didn't like the idea of letting a student into his copy room, but this was a better alternative than handing the machine over to the Honor Board, as in past elections. He wanted to be nearby when the last vote was tallied.

Lincoln wasn't happy with the arrangement either, especially since it meant that he'd have to skip lunch. (He was one of the few students who actually liked the cafeteria food.) But he saw this sacrifice as part of the job. At least, that's what he told himself as he headed to the main office. He was so busy trying to ignore the aroma of beef and mashed potatoes that he walked right into Megan Feldman.

"Oh, sorry," he said. "I wasn't paying attention to where I was going."

Megan pulled a strand of hair from her face. "No problem. Actually, I was looking for you."

"Really?" Lincoln replied, his voice suddenly a deep baritone.

"Since you're in charge of the election process, let me run something by you. I've been talking to the cheerleaders about starting a new tradition — having the newly elected officers take the floor for the first dance at the formal. Kind of like what the president does at the Inaugural Ball." Their eyes met. "Do you think that's a good idea?"

Sweat trickled down Lincoln's arm. "Um . . . I think that's an excellent idea," he said.

"Since the Honor Board is responsible for the election process, you'll have to take part in the first dance as well." She stepped closer to him. "You *are* coming to the formal tonight, right?"

"I . . . I didn't plan on it."

"Why not?"

He gulped. "I don't have a date."

Megan patted his arm. "That's okay. When it comes time for the inaugural dance, you can just dance with me."

"What do you mean, it's broken?!" Lincoln said, his voice as loud as the groaning, grating sound emanating from the scoring machine. "It can't be broken!"

Mrs. Goldman turned off the machine. "Looks like you'll have to wait until Monday to announce the results."

"Maybe I can score the ballots by hand."

"I doubt Dr. Kelsey will allow you to miss class just to count the ballots."

"Maybe the office helpers can chip in. That kid Bradley — he's pretty dependable."

She shook her head. "Our office helpers have more important things to do than score election ballots."

"But the cheerleaders . . . There's a new tradition. . . ." He furrowed his brow. "You said this was a new machine, right? Can we get the old one back?"

"Lincoln, I don't think —"

"Please." His voice cracked. "This is really, really important."

She sighed. "Let me get the number." She slipped on her glasses and peered at the label on the machine. "Don't get your hopes up. It's almost impossible to get something delivered before the end of the day. Especially on a Friday."

After she jotted the number on the back of her hand, Mrs. Goldman returned to her desk with Lincoln a few steps behind. Bradley looked up from the counter (where he was engaged in the all-important task of color-coding paper clips) but didn't speak as Mrs. Goldman updated Dr. Kelsey on the status of the machine. Then she called the leasing company.

"Hello," she said. "This is Alicia Goldman from Maplewood. . . . That's right, you guys delivered a machine to us today. It seems that the machine is broken. . . . Yes, I understand, but perhaps you could return the old one." She nodded as someone on the other end of the phone spoke, then put her hand over the receiver. "He's checking with the delivery person now."

As Lincoln crossed his fingers and toes, he thought about Megan's tousled hair, dimpled cheeks, and perfect smile. He could almost see himself dancing with her. That was a lot better than going to Stewart Hogan's house to play *Ultimate Fantasy IV*. Stewart couldn't find a date to the formal either.

"Oh, I see," Mrs. Goldman said, snapping Lincoln back to the present. "You can't deliver it until six o'clock? Okay, thank you."

She hung up the phone and turned to a shell-shocked Lincoln. "It looks like we're going to have to wait until Monday."

Bradley cleared his throat. "Why can't they deliver it tonight?" he asked. "Everyone will be here for the formal."

"Not me," Mrs. Goldman said. "And neither will Ms. Appleton."

"But once it's here, I can handle running the machine myself," Lincoln said. "It's my duty — no, my responsibility — to tally those votes. People are depending on me."

Mrs. Goldman rolled her eyes as she looked at Dr. Kelsey. He frowned, tapped the rim of his reading glasses, then finally nodded. "Go ahead and call them back," Dr. Kelsey said. "I'll sign for the machine tonight."

Dr. Kelsey returned to his office, and Lincoln left to find Megan. Mrs. Goldman picked up the phone. "I swear, everyone at that company seems familiar," she said as she punched the keypad. "If I didn't know better, I'd say the person on the other end of the phone sounded just like one of the Greene boys."

Jackson Sends a MESSAGE

Keith couldn't help but smile as he walked — no, strutted — to the office. It was minutes before the last bell, and all the candidates had been asked to meet with Dr. Kelsey. This could only mean one thing. He was about to be named the next Student Council president.

He paused at the door and took a few deep breaths. He wanted to compose himself to make sure he looked confident. Regal. Presidential.

He turned as he heard footsteps behind him. "Hey, Gaby," he said. He opened the door for her. "Ladies first. It's the least your president can do."

She huffed. "Isn't that a bit cocky?"

"Not cocky. Confident. It's one of my many presidential features."

They stepped into Dr. Kelsey's office, joining the candidates for the other offices. Keith had to stand close to Gaby so they could all fit inside. Not that he minded.

"I think that's everyone," Dr. Kelsey said. He wiped his nose, then stuffed the linen handkerchief into his jacket pocket. "How many of you are attending the formal?" After everyone raised their hands, he said, "Good. Because due to a malfunction with the scoring machine, we won't be able to announce the results until tonight."

Keith tensed up. "What's the problem?"

"The district supplied a faulty machine this morning. They'll deliver our old one back to us this evening."

"But —"

"It's under control. Lincoln Miller will scan the ballots himself."

"But . . . but . . ."

"Okay, see you all tonight," Dr. Kelsey said, waving his hand dismissively.

As everyone filed out of the room, Keith remained in place, staring at the top of Dr. Kelsey's head.

"Close your mouth," Gaby said as she pushed past him. "You're drooling all over your presidential features."

Keith slammed his fist into his locker, making the metal ring throughout the hallway.

Wilton took a timid step toward him. "Dude, calm down. You'll find out tonight."

"Jackson's behind this." He hit the locker again. "Are you sure you and Victor cleaned everything out of that shed?"

Wilton looked around. "Maybe we shouldn't be talking about this out in the open."

"Did you get it all or not?"

Wilton quickly nodded. "We got everything," he whispered. "The ballots. The machine. All the keys."

"Are you sure?" He undid his padlock and opened the door. "You have to be absolutely —"

Keith froze — not blinking, not even breathing — as he gazed inside his locker.

It was empty, except for a lone ballot.

Keith grabbed the ballot and stared at the message written across it.

> Keep it. There are 371 more
> where this came from.

Contrary to the words scrawled across the walls of the boys' bathroom, Dr. Kelsey was indeed a smart man. He hadn't wanted to say anything in front of the students, especially Keith, but the problems with the scanner stunk of Jackson Greene.

Dr. Kelsey leaned back in his chair and slipped his hands behind his head. He could call off the election, delay things until Monday.

Or he could let things unfold. Roderick Sinclair's generous donation had already been deposited into his account. The way he saw it, he had little to lose and everything to gain — like the chance to expel a certain student.

He'd caught Jackson Greene once before. How hard would it be to catch him again?

LAST-SECOND STUFF

As soon as Megan entered the back room of Basilone's Lock and Key, she made a beeline for Jackson Greene.

"What's wrong?" he asked.

"Don't you feel a little guilty?"

"About what? Rigging the machine? Breaking into the copy room?"

Megan shook her head. "I'm fine with that. But we're not just breaking a few stupid rules. We're leading people on. *I'm* leading someone on." She shuddered. "It's a bit disgusting."

"Lincoln?"

She nodded.

"Think about it this way," Jackson began, spinning his pencil between his fingers. "You're not leading Lincoln on — you're just promising to dance with him. Nothing more, nothing less. You like him enough to dance with him, right?"

Megan thought for a second. "Sure. I'd dance with just about anyone."

There was a loud crash at the other end of the room.

"My fault," Hashemi yelled as he knelt to pick up some scattered electronics. "Just dropped a laptop battery on my foot. But I'm okay. No broken bones. I'm still in good enough shape to dance tonight. . . . You know, if anyone wants to dance . . . Not that I'm trying to *force* anyone to dance with me . . ."

Jackson leaned into Megan. "Since you like dancing so much, maybe you could find time to dance with a few other guys as well."

Megan rolled her eyes. "Boys. So cute, yet so stupid."

Jackson called the group together. "Hash, you want to explain how we're going to communicate tonight — assuming nothing's broken?"

"Nothing's broken," he said. "Like I said, my foot —"

"I was talking about the equipment."

"Oh, of course. So yes, thanks to Megan, we have a state-of-the-art communications system. It's designed to ignore background noise and amplify the voice speaking into the microphone. I'll be able to monitor you all and patch you in to the other team members." Hashemi held up a small earpiece. "I found these at The Spy Zone. The earbud is tiny, hardly detectible. And this . . ." He waved a small square of black plastic. "This is the microphone. It'll be linked via Bluetooth to a cell phone you'll carry in your pocket." Hashemi tucked the microphone in the breast pocket of his shirt. "Bradley and I tested them out a few minutes ago. They work perfectly, and the battery will last at least six hours."

"Phones?" Jackson asked.

Hashemi pulled a thin flip phone from his back pocket. "It isn't fancy, but it'll get the job done."

Samuel looked at his brother. "You know what will happen if Kelsey finds you with a cell phone."

Jackson smirked. "Then I guess he'd better not find it."

"And what am I supposed to do with the microphone?" Megan stood and poked Hashemi's breast pocket. "I'm wearing a dress. It's strapless."

Bradley raised his hand, but after Jackson flashed him a look, he dropped his arm. "Maybe Megan doesn't need one. We'll know where she is," Bradley said.

Jackson shook his head. "We all have to stay in contact. It's too risky."

"Well, I'm not changing my outfit," she said.

"Maybe I can make it into some type of necklace," Hashemi offered. "I just need to get my hands on some copper wire to —"

"Hold up," Megan said. "Let me see the microphone again."

After Hashemi handed her the microphone, she bounced it in the palm of her hand and gauged its weight. "It's pretty small. . . . I think I can find somewhere to hide it."

Hashemi frowned. "The microphone has to be close to your mouth in order to pick up your voice."

"I know," she replied.

"So you can't put it in your purse or anything like that," he continued.

"She knows," Jackson said.

"So where are you going to hide it?" Hashemi asked. "If your dress is strapless, you won't have anywhere close enough to your mouth to put it. . . ."

And then, finally, Hashemi got it.

"The things I do for you guys," Megan mumbled. "Where's your bathroom, Ray? Let's see if this'll work."

Ray led her to the bathroom. Hashemi's face was still as red as spaghetti sauce when he returned. "Smooth, Hashemi," Ray said, trying not to laugh. "Real smooth."

Hashemi buried his head in his hands. "I am such an idiot."

"Focus, Hash." Jackson sat back down. "Will you be able to track us?"

Hashemi nodded. "I'll be in the van. Watching your every move. And hiding from Megan."

Jackson gave him a sympathetic pat on the back, then turned to Charlie. "Do you know if Megan coordinated with the cheerleaders and Mrs. McCoy?"

"Each candidate's gift will be waiting for them when they arrive."

"And the Robot in Disguise?"

Samuel stood. "Me and Ray have it covered."

"One last thing," Jackson said. "Everyone remember the signal for a Code Red?"

He waited until everyone nodded. "Good. Meet you at the school at six." He tucked his pencil behind his ear. "Let's go steal an election."

a GROUP EFFORT

Jackson walked up the long, cracked concrete path to the gymnasium. His brother's three-piece charcoal suit was nearly a perfect fit. His shoes were so polished that he could see his reflection (he'd checked), and his cuff links shined in the evening light. Although his brother had tried to convince him to wear a bow tie, Jackson remained faithful to his own tastes, and instead wore a striped red tie.

One look at Charlie's neon-blue bow tie and vest convinced Jackson that he had made the right choice.

"Like it?" Charlie asked. "Dad let me borrow it."

"It's a classic," Jackson said. He fiddled with his cuff. "So how does she look?"

"Good. Perfect. She'll have Lincoln eating out of her —"

"I wasn't asking about Megan."

"Oh? *Oh.*" Charlie glanced toward the open doors of the gym. "She's inside. Why don't you see for yourself?"

"In a second." He pulled his sleeve back over his cuff. "I kind of lied when I said you were a floater. I need you to run point."

Charlie felt himself jerk backward. "Wait. . . . *What*?"

"You're right about Kelsey. He'll be on me all night. You have to run the team."

Charlie waited for the smile to crack on Jackson's face. It never came. "Why didn't you tell me this before?"

"Hashemi's not the only one who performs better under pressure." He punched Charlie's shoulder. "Now, if you'll excuse me. . . ."

Jackson left a wide-eyed Charlie de la Cruz on the sidewalk and entered the gym. To the left, members of the Botany Club sat at a foldout table underneath a sign that said FLOWERS FOR THE CANDIDATES.

Although Gaby stood at the table with her back to Jackson, he recognized her immediately. She wore a long flowing dress — jet black with touches of silver and lace. Her hair was curled and pinned to the top of her head, showing off her long, graceful neck.

"Need help with that?" he asked as she picked up one of the corsages.

Gaby hesitated, then allowed him to take the corsage. "You look nice."

"So do you. But you always look nice." He focused on the corsage, working to fasten it to her dress without touching too much of her skin. Stealing the Riggins Middle School goat had been less nerve-wracking.

"Maybe you should let me do that," Winnie, one of the Botany Club members, said.

Jackson flashed Gaby an inquisitive look.

"No, it's okay," Gaby said, her cheeks warming. "I think he's almost got it."

He finished pinning the corsage without sticking her or himself. "Where's Omar?"

She nodded toward the lone basketball goal that remained unfolded. A handful of boys stood underneath, while Omar, in full tuxedo — cummerbund and all — slipped and slid across the floor, trying his best to dribble in his loafers.

"Maybe the tux will improve his jump shot."

"Jackson . . ."

"I'll be nice. I promise." He stepped away and looked at the corsage. "It goes well with your dress."

"A red chrysanthemum." She glanced at his lapel. "And you're wearing a flower as well?"

"It's called a pimpernel."

"Scarlet?"

"Maybe I just wanted to match you." He smiled. "And let's be honest — if you're going to wear a pimpernel, it may as well be scarlet."

She waved toward the table. "Why do I get the feeling you're behind this?"

"Like I said — you deserve flowers."

Gaby glanced toward the basketball goal, where Omar had just launched a missile that ricocheted off the rim, almost taking out the punch bowl. "What would have happened if *he* bought me a corsage?"

"I guess you would have had to make a choice."

Gaby stepped closer to Jackson. "Just what are you saying, Jackson Greene?"

Before he could respond, Jackson heard a beep in his ear, then the crackle of static. Finally, a voice came through the earpiece. "This is Hashemi, checking in. Jackson, you there?"

Jackson sighed. "Let's talk later," he said to Gaby. "There are . . . too many people around."

He left her standing by the practically empty flower table, her face a mixture of surprise and confusion, and walked off to a secluded corner of the gym. He unbuttoned his jacket and patted his vest pockets, just to be sure the cell phone and mic were hidden from view. "Charlie, this is your baby. Run us through."

"Uh, okay," Charlie said, his voice quiet but steady. "Everyone check in."

"I'm inside the gym," Jackson said. "Waiting for mark number one."

"Bradley here. Walking toward the main office. Looking for mark number two. I also passed by Megan. She probably can't respond, but she's with the cheerleaders."

"Hashemi, does the tracking work?" Charlie asked, his voice louder.

The team heard the clicking of keys through their earpieces. "Affirmative. We're up and running. I can see you all." Hashemi cleared his throat. "I bet you're all so comfortable. Standing up. Able to stretch. Able to move."

Charlie groaned. "Hashemi . . ."

"I mean, I'm not complaining. Why go to a dance, where there are girls and music, when I can sit on a milk crate in a van with a hot laptop balanced on my knees?"

Charlie laughed. "I hate to interrupt your plea for sympathy, but mark number one is approaching the gym. Jackson, any last words?"

Jackson slipped off his jacket and threw it over his shoulder. "Hash, tell Ray to deliver the package."

While a certain gold-toothed, sunglass-wearing deliveryman walked toward the main office with a not-a-Scantron machine, Keith entered the gym with Alyssa Robbins by his side. She didn't really like him, but he was in eighth grade and was a jock. She was a seventh grader and wanted to be noticed. It was a match made in heaven.

"Hello, Gaby," Keith said when they reached the flower table. "Whose idea was it for the flowers?"

Gaby glanced toward the corner, then forced a smile. "You know how good ideas are. It's hard to pin them on one person. It's more of a group effort." Her gaze dropped to the table. "I'm sure there's one here for you."

"Of course there is," Mrs. McCoy said, walking over to Gaby and Keith. "I see you found yours, Gabriela. And Keith, here's yours."

The red rose, with its large and crisp petals, looked massive in Mrs. McCoy's hands. The boutonniere was accented with baby's breath and green leatherleaf, but the rose was the center of attention.

"It's hypoallergenic," she said, stretching her hand toward him. "That means you won't be allergic to it."

Keith cleared his throat and reminded himself to talk with some bass in his voice. "I know what *hypoallergenic* means."

He was lying, of course.

Alyssa pointed to Keith's chest. "What about the boutonniere I gave you?"

Keith's eyes went from the flower in Mrs. McCoy's hands to the other flowers on the table. The other candidates' flowers paled in size and color. Their flowers were adequate. His was tailored for a king. Or a president.

"I'm sorry, Alyssa," he said. "But I have to wear this one. I wouldn't want to be different from the other candidates."

Bradley stood in the office, holding a rose similar to Keith's. "Mrs. McCoy asked me to bring this. She said it's hypoallergenic. That means you won't be allergic to it."

Dr. Kelsey took the flower. "I know what *hypoallergenic* means."

He was lying, of course.

Bradley began to walk out, but stopped and snapped his fingers. "Did they ever deliver the scoring machine?"

"They just dropped it off," Dr. Kelsey replied, fumbling with the flower. Finally, he pinned it to his jacket, proud that he only stuck himself twice. "I need to find Lincoln so I can get back to the formal. I want to keep my eye on things out there."

"Want me to find him and send him this way?"

"Are you sure you don't mind?" Dr. Kelsey sucked on his thumb. "You should be dancing. Having fun."

Bradley opened the door. "I promise, I'm having the time of my life right now."

THE KEYS TO THE CRIME

As the gym filled with awkward boys and pretty girls, the DJ began pumping music through the speakers. From his corner, Jackson saw Bradley talk with Lincoln, then lead him out of the gym. He checked his watch and moved to a new corner, and tried to ignore how close Gaby and Omar danced to each other.

"Decide to be a wallflower?" Keith asked as Jackson passed by the snack table en route to another corner.

Jackson nodded at Keith's boutonniere. "That's a big rose. It matches your ego."

Keith glared. "What do you have planned? What are you trying to pull?"

"I have no idea what you're talking about."

Jackson walked away, but Keith followed. "Even if you somehow got your hands on the Scantron machine, there's no way you could have rigged it in a day," Keith said. "According to Victor, it took the butterball five days to modify the old one."

"You're right. There's no way Hashemi could learn from his mistakes and rig a scoring machine within that time frame. It's clearly impossible," Jackson said, yawning. "And like I said, it's not a Scantron."

Keith could feel doubt eating away at his confidence. "Even then, there's no way you could switch out the —"

"Relax, Keith." Jackson patted his shoulder. "I'm sure you and Kelsey have it under control. You thought of everything, right?" He winked. "May the best woman win."

Jackson strutted off, leaving Keith with his mouth gaping open for the second time that day. He finally snapped it shut and marched toward the dance floor. He grabbed Wilton, mumbled a brief apology to Wilton's date, and dragged him away.

"I knew it!" Keith said, stopping at the snack table. "Jackson rigged the machine. Did Victor rebubble all those ballots like I asked?"

Wilton rubbed his arm where Keith had grabbed him. "He wasn't happy about it, but he did it. His hand looks like it got caught in a trash compactor."

"Like I care about Victor Cho. He should be glad I'm letting him keep his Chess Team." He scanned the gym for Jackson Greene, but he had disappeared. "Go get the ballots and meet me in the atrium in ten minutes. We can hide behind that row of potted plants."

"Keith —"

"I've got the keys to the main office and the copy room. All we have to do is wait for Lincoln to leave the room, then we'll sneak in and replace the real ballots with ours. We'll run the same con that Jackson was trying to pull — call for a recount and win once they hand-count the ballots."

"But why? Kelsey guaranteed you a win. What more do you want?"

"You think I trust Kelsey? There's no way I'm leaving this election up to him." Keith grabbed Wilton's arm again. "So come on —"

"No." He shrugged Keith off. "Go on your own if you want. The ballots are in my gym locker. But I'm not sneaking into the office. I'm through with all your crazy schemes."

Keith reeled back. "You're supposed to be my right-hand man."

"No, I'm supposed to be your treasurer," Wilton said. "But maybe I'll be Gaby's."

Lincoln sat in the copy room, the green plastic seat hard and cold beneath him, and stared as one ballot after another slipped through the machine. It was akin to watching water drip from a rusty faucet. In the middle of the night. After being awake for forty-nine hours.

But Lincoln wasn't going to complain. This was his job. His responsibility. Even though he wasn't allowed to touch the machine, other than to load the feeding tray. Even though Dr. Kelsey had forbidden him from printing out the scoring results. Even though every minute spent in the copy room was a minute away from Megan Feldman.

The key to the copy room rested on the table next to the scoring machine. It was Dr. Kelsey's personal copy — he had demanded that Lincoln keep it in his sight at all times. And that's exactly what Lincoln did, letting his gaze bounce between the key and the machine. He was so busy staring that at first he didn't hear the tapping.

It wasn't until banging replaced the tapping that Lincoln shook himself from his slouch, grabbed the key, and raced out of the room. Once he saw who was standing beyond the main office windows, he ran faster.

"Hey, Megan," he said after he cracked open the office door. "What are you —"

"I've been looking all over for you." A charcoal-gray jacket rested loosely on her shoulders. "You promised me a dance, remember?"

Lincoln wished he had popped a mint before opening the door. "Um . . . Yes. But the results aren't done yet."

"How much longer? The DJ promised to play my favorite song."

"I don't know. . . ."

"Let's find out," Megan said, already pushing her way inside the office.

Lincoln followed her down the hallway. "I don't think this is a good idea. Dr. Kelsey said —"

"What? You think I'll tamper with the results?"

"No, of course not." Lincoln opened the copy room door for her.

Megan put her hands on her hips as she peered at the ballots. "What do you think? Maybe halfway though?"

"Yeah. Maybe." Her eyes were just too much — too clear, too crisp, too beautiful — to stare at, so Lincoln focused on the jacket around her perfect frame, and the small red flower tucked into the buttonhole on the lapel.

"Come on," she said. "Load up the rest of the ballots, and let's go."

"But I'm supposed to —"

"It's not like you need to be here the entire time." She held out her hand, palm up. "Come on. Give me the key and load up those ballots."

"But —"

"Lincoln. Key. Ballots. Now."

As he dropped the key into her hand, he hoped it wasn't too sweaty. He hastily loaded the remaining ballots onto the feeding tray, then followed her out of the office. He watched her lock the copy room door, then he checked to make sure that the main office door locked behind them.

Megan slid the copy room key into her jacket pocket, then slipped her arm into his. "I hope they haven't already played the song."

He took two steps, then stopped. "Um . . . Maybe you'd better give me the key. Just in case you forget."

She reached into her pocket. "Sorry. What was I thinking?" She placed the cold, dry key in his hand. "I'd hate to lose that. No telling what would happen if the wrong person got their hands on it."

Lincoln nodded and stuffed the key into his pocket. As they turned down the hall toward the gym, he was so intent on not tripping, on not making a fool of himself, on not sweating all over Megan's arm, he didn't hear the hushed footsteps of one of Maplewood's finest student-athletes carrying a book bag full of ballots across the atrium, the jingle of two keys in his pocket.

Lincoln wanted to enjoy himself. To be happy. To have a night to remember.

So did Keith.

aLL LOCKED UP

"They're on the move," Hashemi said.

"We've got a problem," Charlie replied, the music blaring all around him. His hands, his face, his entire body felt weighed down with sweat. "Jackson can't shake Kelsey. He's trying to be incognito, but he's following Jackson like a shadow." He started to move toward the center of the room. "Maybe I can make a diversion —"

"Negative," Jackson mumbled into his vest. He dropped to his feet and pretended to adjust his shoe. "Charlie, you have the equipment. You can't be tied up. Think of something else." Just as Kelsey approached, Jackson stood up and continued on.

Charlie's eyes burnt from the sweat pouring down his forehead. "Megan, can you stall?"

A few seconds later, Megan's voice floated over the boys' earpieces. "Hold up a second. These heels are killing me."

As Lincoln mumbled a reply, Charlie said, "Bradley, I need you to make a diversion."

"What?"

"Do something. Anything. I don't care."

"But —"

"Just make it happen. Now."

Bradley sighed. "Fine, I'm on it." He quickly crossed the dance floor, passing Dr. Kelsey and Mr. Garcia, one of the unfortunate teachers drafted into serving as a chaperone. He hovered by the snack table and waited as Omar poured himself a glass of strawberry punch. Then, right as Mickey Mac hit the highest of high notes in the Sk8tr Boiz's new number-one single, "U R 2 Much 4 Me," Bradley closed his eyes and leapt into the table.

Dr. Kelsey peeled his gaze away from Jackson as the sound of shattering glass echoed throughout the gym. "What in the world . . . ?"

"I think someone tripped," Mr. Garcia said, pointing to the lanky boy laid out in the corner, his hands cupped around his nose. Omar stood beside him, his suit drenched with red punch. What remained of the snack table lay scattered across the floor. "From the way it looks, he fell pretty hard." He started toward the student, but stopped once he noticed that Dr. Kelsey wasn't following. "Dr. Kelsey? Are you coming?"

Dr. Kelsey took one final look at Jackson Greene, still standing in his corner. "Of course. Let's see what's going on."

As soon as Dr. Kelsey turned toward Bradley, Jackson bolted toward the gymnasium doors. "Charlie?"

"Already on my way. I'll meet you at the office."

Jackson burst out of the side doors of the gymnasium, almost running into Megan and Lincoln.

"There you are," Megan said, already slipping off the jacket. "I was so cold. Thank you for letting me borrow this."

"No problem," Jackson said. He nodded at Lincoln, took the jacket, and kept moving.

Charlie stood outside the main office, a small black bag hanging from his shoulder. "How about Bradley, taking one for the team?" He elbowed Jackson. "I picked him, you know."

"Focus today. Gloat tomorrow." Jackson slipped the bump key into the lock and opened the door. As soon as it shut behind them, they raced toward the copy room.

Keith paused as he heard voices outside the door. He had just started replacing the real ballots with his doctored ones. It was taking longer than he expected — he hadn't counted on so many students voting for Gaby. (And by "so many," he meant "everyone.") But now, as the voices got closer, he worried that he'd taken too long. He looked around the room, hoping that a window would miraculously appear. Then he noticed the closet.

Ballots in hand, he dove into the closet and yanked the

door shut. Seconds later, he heard the copy room door creak open.

"Switch out just enough to tip it in Gaby's favor. And hurry. Lincoln won't be dancing forever."

Keith stiffened. He knew that voice.

Jackson Greene.

So Jackson hadn't rigged the machine, he thought. *Jackson was doing exactly what he planned to do.*

He almost stepped out of the closet, but stopped himself. This was even better. After Jackson finished with the ballots, he'd swap them out with his.

Focus today, he told himself, repeating a line that he'd heard somewhere before. *Gloat tomorrow.*

So he sat back down and listened as Jackson noisily shuffled around the room.

Finally, after what felt like hours, he heard Jackson say, "Okay, I think we're good."

A few seconds later, the door clicked shut.

Keith cautiously exited the closet. Not wanting to spend any more time in the room, he grabbed all the ballots from the machine, removed roughly 80 percent, then shuffled his doctored ones into the pile. He placed half in the queue to run through the machine and the others in the pile that had already been scored. If it turned out that Gaby won, he'd just call for a recount.

He started the machine again, paused to straighten his boutonniere, then walked to the door.

He inserted his key and —

Nothing.

The key didn't turn.

The knob didn't turn.

The door didn't, wouldn't, couldn't open.

Keith Sinclair was locked inside the copy room.

a NOSE FOR THE TRUTH

Once Dr. Kelsey got Bradley to his feet and sent a student to get a mop and some towels, he turned back to the corner of the gym.

Jackson Greene had disappeared.

He grabbed his walkie-talkie. "Mr. James, where are you?"

The line crackled alive. "Outside in the golf cart," Mr. James said. "I'm, um . . . surveying the parking lot."

"I need you inside. We need to find Jackson Greene."

"Did he do something wrong?" Mr. James asked.

Dr. Kelsey snorted. "He's Jackson Greene. He's always up to something, and with all the strangeness going on today, I wouldn't put it past him to be involved."

"Maybe he just went to the restroom?"

Dr. Kelsey started toward the gymnasium doors, but stopped when he saw Lincoln slow-dancing with Megan. "Mr. Garcia, as soon as this song ends, please escort Mr. Miller to the main office. I'll meet you there in five minutes, as soon as I walk the halls."

Dr. Kelsey zipped through each hallway, moving faster than a man of his age, size, and health should. When he reached the main office, he couldn't even acknowledge Mr. Garcia or Lincoln — he was too out of breath.

He wiped the moisture from his forehead and raised the walkie-talkie. "Did you . . . find him?"

"No, sir," Mr. James replied.

"Check the second floor. I know he's here." Dr. Kelsey stretched his hand toward Lincoln. "My key."

His hand shaking like a leaf in a hurricane, Lincoln dropped the key into Dr. Kelsey's hand. "I'm sorry. It's just . . . Megan wanted to dance. And I —"

"Are the results finalized?" a new voice asked.

Dr. Kelsey turned around to see Gabriela and Charlie de la Cruz standing behind him. "When we saw Lincoln walking back, we assumed that the ballots had been tallied," Gaby said.

"Let's go check." Dr. Kelsey pulled a small ring of keys from his jacket pocket. He slipped the copy room key back on the key ring, then fished out the key to the main office. Although he didn't want all these students in his copy room, he also wanted to keep tabs on Charlie de la Cruz. If Jackson really was up to something, Charlie was probably in on it as well.

He unlocked the door. "Mr. Garcia, see if you can help Mr. James find Jackson Greene."

Gaby noticed Charlie flinch at the mention of Jackson's name. "Something wrong?" she whispered.

Charlie grinned so wide, his face practically disappeared

behind his smile. "No problem. Not at all," he said, following Dr. Kelsey into the office.

At the copy room door, Dr. Kelsey couldn't help but notice how shiny and sharp the key was — nothing like the dull, dirty one he'd been carrying around for years. He wondered if Lincoln had cleaned it for him while he was waiting.

He rubbed his jaw as he looked at the ballots pouring through the machine. "Should be just about done."

"So it's just about done?" Charlie repeated loudly, his mouth directed at his tie.

"Um . . . Yes," Dr. Kelsey said, frowning.

Charlie smiled. "Good. I can't wait to see the results."

Lincoln returned to his hard plastic seat. Dr. Kelsey planted himself in front of the scoring machine. Charlie and Gaby leaned against the wall. And they waited.

Just as the last ballot ran through the machine, Bradley appeared at the door, his shirt covered in red punch and potato chip crumbs. He held a bouquet of flowers in his hands, as far away from his body as his arms would allow. "These were just delivered," he said, entering the room. "They're for you, Gaby."

"Me?"

Bradley handed her the bouquet. "There's a card."

Gaby took the flowers and breathed them in. She didn't open the card. There was no need.

Suddenly aware that all eyes were on her, she pointed to the now-silent machine. "So who won?"

Dr. Kelsey punched a few buttons and waited for the machine to print out the results. He had planned to lie now and swap the report out later with the doctored one in his office, but he was surprised to find that this wouldn't be necessary. "I'm sorry," he said, looking at the sheet. "It looks like Keith won."

Lincoln sprang from his seat. "I'll need a copy of the printout for documentation purposes." He straightened his tie. After the official announcement, maybe he'd have time for one more dance with Megan.

Charlie pushed himself off the wall. "Are you sure Keith won?"

Gaby smiled at her brother. "It's okay. You can't win all the time. I'm sure Keith will be a good president."

It stung even to say the words.

Dr. Kelsey opened his mouth to offer what he hoped would be words of encouragement and inspiration.

Instead he sneezed, barely covering his mouth before spraying Charlie and Gaby.

"I'm sorry," he said, wiping his nose. "I didn't mean —"

He sneezed again.

Then Lincoln sneezed.

Then Charlie sneezed.

Then Bradley sneezed twice in a row, loudly, hard enough to make his nose hurt.

And then —

Someone else sneezed.

Gaby, Charlie, Bradley, Lincoln, and Dr. Kelsey looked at each other. Then they turned toward the closet.

Another sneeze.

Dr. Kelsey ran to the closet. There was no superintendent to save the boy this time. He had finally gotten the best of Jackson Greene.

Except —

"Keith?" Dr. Kelsey mumbled.

Keith cowered behind a box, his hands full of crumpled-up ballots.

"Congratulations," Charlie said, snapping a picture with the MAPE. "You won the election. For a minute, anyway."

"What are you . . . ?" Dr. Kelsey scratched his head. "How did you . . . ?"

Keith sneezed again.

"Let me see those flowers." Dr. Kelsey took the bouquet from Gaby and ripped open the card.

> Aren't you glad you aren't
> allergic to these?
> — J. G.

Dr. Kelsey thrust the flowers back into Gaby's hands and turned on his walkie-talkie. "Someone find Jackson Greene!"

"I found him, sir," Mr. James said, his voice loud over the static. "He was by the eighth-grade lockers. Said he was looking for a bathroom."

"Bring him here," Dr. Kelsey said into the walkie-talkie. Then he looked at Keith, ballots spilling from his pockets. "Actually, take Jackson to the gym. I'll meet you there in a few minutes. I've got something to deal with first."

"He says he has to use the bathroom."

"Mr. James, do not let that boy out of your sight." He pocketed his walkie-talkie, then grabbed Keith's arm.

Keith struggled to get out of Kelsey's grip. "It wasn't my fault. It was Jackson. He was here. He tricked me."

"Rat," Gaby and Charlie mumbled at the same time.

"Wait," Keith said. "I can explain."

Lincoln picked up the crumpled ballots from the floor — each with a vote for Gaby. "Keith Sinclair, in accordance with the Maplewood Honor Code and the Student Council bylaws, I hereby nullify these election results and strip you of the right to run as a candidate in any future Maplewood Student Council elections."

"So this means Gaby won, right?" Charlie asked.

"Technically, there will have to be a formal investigation. But based on the number of ballots for Gaby, I think it's safe to say that she would have won this election in a landslide." Lincoln began organizing the evidence. "You'll all be witnesses, of course. You too, Dr. Kelsey."

"A formal investigation?" Keith gulped. "You won't . . . You can't —"

"Of course I can," Lincoln said. "It's my job. It's in the bylaws."

a BYSTANDER NO MORE

Lincoln, Charlie, Bradley, and Gaby remained quiet as Dr. Kelsey shooed them out of the main office and locked the door behind them.

"Congratulations," Lincoln said to Gaby as he shook her hand. "I'm looking forward to working with you this year."

Gaby smiled and watched as Lincoln walked back toward the gym. As soon as he disappeared around the corner, Charlie cleared his throat and brought his hand to his ear.

"Megan, what's going on in there?" Charlie asked.

"Mr. James has Jackson by the flower table. Looks like Jackson is trying to get away, but Mr. James isn't budging."

"Jackson, if you can hear me, stretch."

Two seconds passed in silence.

"Megan, is he stretching?" Charlie asked.

"Yep."

"Crap," Charlie said. "If he can hear me —"

"— then that means he wasn't able to get rid of the phone," Bradley said.

"Okay, what's going on?" Gaby asked, one hand on her hip, the other holding her bouquet. "What are you guys up to?"

Ignoring his sister, Charlie focused on the wall and forced himself to take deep breaths. "Okay, Jackson, stretch again if you still have the main office and copy room keys on you."

Two more seconds passed, then —

"Double crap," Megan said.

Gaby poked Bradley. "Are you talking with an earpiece?"

Bradley nodded. "Hashemi hooked us up with these earpieces and microphones in our pockets and —"

"Give me yours."

"But —"

"Bradley. Earpiece."

He reluctantly pulled out the earpiece.

"I hope you washed your ears today," she said, sticking it in her ear. "Where's the microphone?"

After Bradley pointed to the upper pocket of his red-stained shirt, she sighed and leaned into him. "Jackson, it's Gaby. Can you —"

She shut up as Dr. Kelsey opened the door, his hand a vise grip on Keith's shoulder. "You stand right here until I get back," he said. "I would lock you in my office, but I think you've been locked in enough rooms tonight." He let go of Keith's shoulder and looked at Gaby, Charlie, and Bradley. "What are you still doing out here?"

"Gaby's just so excited about being elected, she needed a little time to compose herself," Charlie said.

Dr. Kelsey narrowed his eyes as his gaze shifted from Charlie to Gaby. "Two minutes. Then I want you back in the gym."

They waited until Dr. Kelsey walked toward the gym. Then they took a few steps away from Keith, who was too busy pouting to really notice them.

"Crap. Crap. Crap," Charlie said. "Kelsey's on his way."

"Mr. James, did you ever see the movie *Star Trek II: The Wrath of Khan*?" Jackson's voice came over the earpiece. "You kind of look like one of the actors. Anyway, it's got so many great lines. . . ."

Charlie froze, his mouth tasting like paste, his feet as heavy as concrete blocks. "You heard him. Code Red."

Gaby shook her head as Bradley began to empty his pockets. "What's going on?"

"Jackson gave the signal," Charlie said. "We toss the phones and destroy the evidence. This way, Kelsey can't catch all of us."

"And what about Jackson?" she asked.

Jackson's voice burst through Gaby's earpiece. "People think it's just a science fiction movie, but it's so much more. There's a great message about how the needs of the many outweigh the needs of the few," he said, still talking to Mr. James. "Or even the one."

Gaby took the cell phone and microphone from Bradley's hands. "Go stall Dr. Kelsey."

"Being bossy must run in your family," Bradley mumbled, but he left.

Gaby spoke into the microphone. "Jackson, if you can still hear me, pat the pocket where you stashed the phone and keys."

"*Ghuy'cha'!*" Megan yelled after a few seconds.

"God bless you," Charlie replied.

"She's speaking in Klingon," Hashemi said. "You don't want to know what it means."

"He's patting in two places," Megan continued. "Left outside jacket pocket. Right pocket on his vest."

"Jackson, if you can, move your earpiece to your left jacket pocket. And make sure your jacket is unbuttoned." Even though Gaby's heart pounded like she'd just run ten suicides across the court, she felt strangely calm. She removed her earpiece. "Charlie, give me your jacket."

"But I didn't iron my shirt."

"Carlito. Jacket. Now."

He took off his jacket. "Bradley's right. You really are bossy."

"Dump this," she said, shoving the electronics into his hands.

"And where are you going?"

"Where else?" she said, running as fast as her heels would allow. "To save Jackson Greene!"

JACKSON GETS A LIFT

As Dr. Kelsey made his way toward the gymnasium, he tried not to get upset at Bradley, who kept jumping in front of him, spouting nonsense about the election and the formal and anything else that seemed to spill from his brain.

Finally, as they entered the gym, he took Bradley by the shoulders and shifted him to one side. "I know you're excited, but I really need to take care of something."

"But, but —"

Dr. Kelsey had already walked off, his eyes locked on Jackson Greene.

"Mr. Greene," he said, tapping the flower table, "I heard you were wandering the hallways."

"I was looking for a bathroom," he said. "I ate too much of the cheese dip . . . needed some privacy, if you know what I mean. Is that a crime?"

"Not for most students," Dr. Kelsey said. "But while you were strolling around the school, I was having the most interesting conversation with Keith Sinclair. He said some shocking things about you and the copy room. Something about hearing you in there."

"I guess rats have supersonic hearing."

"Please empty your pockets."

"Isn't this against my student rights or something?"

"Perhaps you've forgotten, but when I allowed you back in school after that unfortunate incident with Ms. Accord, you and your parents signed a form allowing me to search you or your locker at any time. And I choose now. So if you don't mind —"

"Jackson! I won!"

Dr. Kelsey turned to see Gabriela de la Cruz running toward Jackson at full speed, her arms stretched wide. She dropped her bouquet on the table, blew past Dr. Kelsey and Mr. James, and leapt into Jackson's arms.

"I can't believe it!" she yelled, spinning Jackson around like a top, her arms tight around his waist. "I'm the next Student Council president!"

"Ms. de la Cruz —"

"And you wouldn't guess what happened to Keith. He —"

"Gabriela de la Cruz!" Dr. Kelsey banged on the table. "You are breaking the public display of affection rule!"

Gaby stopped spinning. She slipped her hands into her jacket pockets and shrugged. "It's just a hug."

"A hug is still considered affection," he said. "You know I have to write this up."

She nodded. "I understand. It's my fault for being so inconsiderate, especially on a night like this. I mean, you already have to explain to the superintendent how Keith

Sinclair broke into the main office and the copy room and tried to throw the election. Keith Sinclair — his father is, what, one of the school's biggest boosters?" She glanced at Charlie as he entered the gym. "Good thing Charlie took a snapshot of Keith in the copy room closet. Between the eyewitness reports and the picture, we have everything we need to explain the situation to the superintendent."

Dr. Kelsey looked from Gaby to Jackson, then back to Gaby. *Maybe she'll make a good president after all*, he thought. "I suppose, for tonight, we can relax the PDA rule." He grunted. "Now as I was saying, Mr. Greene, if you don't mind . . ."

Jackson slowly emptied his pockets.

One comb.

One money clip.

A pack of Life Savers, half-eaten.

One pencil.

One notepad.

And a small, square, black box.

"What's this?" Dr. Kelsey asked, eyeing the box.

Jackson shrugged. "I think it's something my brother left in the suit. Maybe a Bluetooth device for his phone?"

"You know you're not allowed to bring a phone onto school property."

"But as you can see, I don't have a phone." He tapped the box. "Really, it's pretty useless without one."

Dr. Kelsey crossed his arms. "Is that everything, Mr. Greene?"

He spread his arms. "You're welcome to check for yourself if you'd like."

Dr. Kelsey took in the flatness of Jackson's pockets and grimaced. "You can collect your things."

Jackson slipped the items back into his suit. "You know, we've had such a tough few months . . . I don't want to end the night on a bad note. . . ." He took a step toward Dr. Kelsey. "And since you said it was okay to hug . . ."

Dr. Kelsey tensed as Jackson gave him a bear hug — his arms barely able to stretch around his body.

"Mr. Greene, please let me go."

"Sorry." Jackson took a step back. "What can I say? I'm overcome with happiness. My ex–best friend just became Student Council president."

Dr. Kelsey, still sulking, turned to Mr. James. "If anyone needs me, I'll be in my office. Keith's father should be here soon." He sighed. Maybe he could book that Tuscan vacation before Roderick Sinclair asked for his money back.

HOW JACKSON GREENE STOLE THE
ELECTION

Jackson waited until Dr. Kelsey and Mr. James exited the gym before elbowing Gaby. "That was the best pull I've ever seen."

She lifted the phone from her pocket. "I learned from a master."

"Thanks —"

"I was talking about Samuel."

Jackson grinned, then nodded at the bouquet that Gaby had placed on the table. "Do you like the Robot in Disguise? I ordered it special, just for you. Chrysanthemums, lilies, juniper, wisteria, ragweed, dandelions. The florist was a little confused when I told her to keep the pollen on the lilies —"

"You knew Keith was in there all along, didn't you? You knew he was hiding."

"It's amazing what you can fit in a boutonniere. All we had to do was pull a couple of GPS chips from Hashemi's cell phone."

"A couple?"

"We didn't want to leave Dr. Kelsey out of the fun," Jackson said. "Though we probably should have given one to Mr. James as well."

"Are you telling her our secrets?" Charlie asked as he arrived with Megan, Bradley, and Hashemi. "What about Rule Number Nine?"

"After the stunt she just pulled, I think we can make her an honorary member of the crew," Jackson said.

"Three cheers for Gang Greene!" Bradley said.

Jackson narrowed his eyes.

"What? I thought it was catchy."

Gaby tapped Jackson's shoulder. "So did I really win? Do you have the real ballots hidden away somewhere?"

"While I'm pretty sure you won, I honestly don't know," Jackson said. "We didn't touch the machine or the ballots while we were in the copy room. We were too busy replacing the lock." He eyed Megan. "Nice job switching the Guttenbabel keys."

"You switched keys?" Gaby frowned. "I don't understand."

"We needed a way to keep Keith in the copy room," Jackson said. "Since a Guttenbabel can be unlocked from both sides, the only way to keep Keith locked in —"

"— was to switch out the deadbolt, which Jackson and I did while Keith hid in the closet." Charlie reached into his — or rather his sister's — jacket pocket and retrieved the original copy room key. "Locks. They have a funny way of not working without the right key."

"So Keith had a way into the room, but not out." Gaby looked at the key in Charlie's hand. "But how did he get the key in the first place?"

"He stole it," Hashemi said. "Victor double-crossed us. Sold us out to Keith. Luckily, Jackson came up with a new plan."

Jackson and Charlie grinned at each other. "You want to tell him or should I?" Jackson asked.

"Let me try." Charlie squared Hashemi in front of him. "Sorry to break this to you, but it was always part of the plan for Victor to pull an Anakin Skywalker."

"What Charlie means to say is, we knew that Victor would double-cross us — or as you might say, turn to the Dark Side. He just needed the incentive, which Keith was happy to provide, and the opportunity." Jackson tried to contain the smile on his face. "Do you really think I'm careless enough to leave all those keys lying around your shed? Do you really think I'm careless enough to show Victor how to *break* into your shed?"

Hashemi wiped his glasses on his tie, then pressed them back onto his face. "So you never planned to sneak into Mr. Pritchard's class and swap out the ballots."

"Nope. Mr. Pritchard's file cabinet isn't the easiest thing to crack." Jackson looked at Gaby. "Not that I've tried or anything."

Hashemi frowned at the others. "Did you two know?"

Both Bradley and Megan nodded.

"So why'd you make me work so hard on rigging the machine?" Hashemi asked Jackson.

"You work better under pressure," Jackson said.

"Seriously, you do," Megan said. "The Tech Club's been waiting all summer for you to finalize that universal translator program."

"Ferengi isn't the easiest language to translate, you know."

"Don't take it too hard," Charlie said, patting Hashemi's shoulder. "I'm sure we'll put those not-a-Scantron machine-rigging talents to good use."

Gaby crossed her arms. "Charlie . . ."

"I'm speaking hypothetically."

"We can discuss all this tomorrow," Jackson said. "Megan, don't you owe someone a dance?"

Megan hooked her arm through Hashemi's. "Come on."

Hashemi's eyes widened. "You want to dance? With me?"

"No, with the other boy who knows how to translate Klingon."

As Megan led Hashemi onto the dance floor, Jackson asked Charlie, "Did you get a picture?"

"Yeah, and it's awesome." Charlie launched the camera app, then handed the MAPE to Jackson. "It'll look great on the front page of the *Herald*."

Jackson admired the photo, pressed a few buttons, then handed it back to Charlie. "It would, but it won't."

Charlie looked at the blank screen. "What did you do?"

"I deleted it."

"What?" Charlie, Gaby, and Bradley all said at the same time.

"That was our only evidence," Charlie said, pawing at the phone.

"Kelsey thinks we have a photo. That's all we need," Jackson said. "And don't break the MAPE. Hash just got it out of beta."

Charlie shook his head. "But . . . but . . ."

"We beat him, Charlie. That's good enough."

Gaby stepped toward this new boy in Jackson Greene's old body. She took a deep breath. "So what about it, Mr. Greene? Are you going to ask me to dance or what?"

Jackson pulled at his tie. "What . . . What about Omar?"

"He left. Someone spilled punch all over his suit."

Bradley coughed. "My bad."

"You took out Omar?" Charlie high-fived Bradley. "Talk about removing the competition."

Gaby ignored Bradley and Charlie, her gaze fixed squarely on Jackson Greene. "I'm waiting."

"I . . . I . . ."

"Dude," Charlie said. "Just tell her."

"Shut up —"

"You're the one who said she was part of the crew. And don't forget Rule Number Seventeen: Once you're part of the crew, you have retroactive access to all past cons."

Jackson snorted. "There is no Rule Number Seventeen."

"I'm running point, remember. My rules, my call." He turned to his sister. "Jackson doesn't know how to dance."

Jackson took Gaby by the arm and led her away from Charlie and Bradley. If he was going to tell the truth, he wanted to tell her face-to-face, his eyes on her eyes, without an audience. "I wanted to ask you to the end-of-year formal, but I wanted to learn how to dance first. And since you're so good at it, I wanted to learn from the best." He offered her a small smile. "Dr. Kelsey had taken Katie's phone. She needed it back, and I needed dance lessons. It sounded like a good idea at the time."

"That's why you agreed to steal her phone?!"

Jackson rubbed the back of his neck. "Samuel also said that running a con with Katie would make you jealous. It was supposed to make you like me more."

Gaby had a good mind to throw her bouquet in Jackson's face. "Jackson Greene, I could slap you right now."

"If it makes you feel better, I never took those lessons."

"Wait — you kissed a girl you didn't like, tried to make me jealous, and almost got kicked out of school — and you *still* didn't learn how to dance?" She looked at the ceiling. "Why are boys so stupid?"

"If we're being technical — just to be clear — I didn't really kiss —"

"Jackson!"

"Okay. I'm sorry for the whole deal with Katie. I'm sorry for never learning how to dance. I'm sorry for being a stupid boy. I'm even sorry for running up the score during the Blitz at the Fitz." He took a step toward her. "Okay?"

She planted her hands on her hips, but Jackson could already see the hint of a smile on her face. "You still broke the rules."

"Yeah, but it was only a small rule. I didn't hijack the election process."

"You broke into the main office."

"Just to fix what Keith had already done."

"You were carrying a cell phone."

"Where?" He opened his jacket. "Last I checked, I didn't have one on me."

She shook her head. "You really have all the answers, don't you, Jackson Greene?" Gaby slipped the jacket off her shoulders. Then she poked Jackson's chest. "My house. Tomorrow. Two o'clock."

He perked up. "Basketball?"

"No. Merengue lessons. Plus, we're going to help Mom make a batch of *pasteles* for dinner."

Jackson's stomach grumbled. "I love your mom's *pasteles*."

"I know." She took his tie and tugged it to the left. "That's why I asked her to cook them."

They stood there, silent, close enough to share the same breath. For a second, Jackson thought that maybe . . . that possibly . . . that perhaps there would be another public display of affection between him and Gabriela de la Cruz.

But before anything could happen, Gaby waved Charlie and Bradley over to join them. She tossed Charlie his jacket and grabbed Bradley's hand. "Let's hit the dance floor."

"But what about Jackson?" Bradley asked.

"There are some lessons that even the Infamous Jackson Greene has to learn the hard way." As she dragged Bradley onto the floor, she called out over her shoulder, "See you tomorrow, Jackson. And you better not be late."

Jackson watched as Gaby fell in step with the music. Bradley struggled to keep up with the beat, always a half-step behind. But at least he was dancing.

"Well, she didn't slam the door in your face this time," Charlie said. He eyed the original copy room key still in his hand. "What should we do with this key? Toss it?"

"A better question is, what should we do with *these* keys?" Jackson reached into his jacket and pulled out a ring of keys that until recently had resided in Dr. Kelsey's pocket. He picked through the keys until he found an oddly shaped silver one.

"Is that —"

"The key to Dr. Kelsey's office? How did that get in my pocket?" Jackson shook the keys. "None of this would have happened if Kelsey hadn't taken that bribe. I'm thinking it's time for a little payback."

"You know he'll change the locks first thing on Monday morning," Charlie said.

"Then it's a good thing we have Sunday open, isn't it?"

And so the Infamous Jackson Greene and his partner, Charlie de la Cruz, exited the gymnasium, whispering in hushed tones, discussing a heist involving the hacking of a certain administrator's computer to quadruple the budgets for the Botany Club, the Tech Club, the *Herald* staff, the Art Geeks, and the Student Council, all using funds from the school's biggest booster. A heist that would somehow include the Honor Board receiving a Scantron machine for its own use. A heist more sophisticated, cunning, ingenious, and beautiful than any job they had ever pulled.

Allegedly.

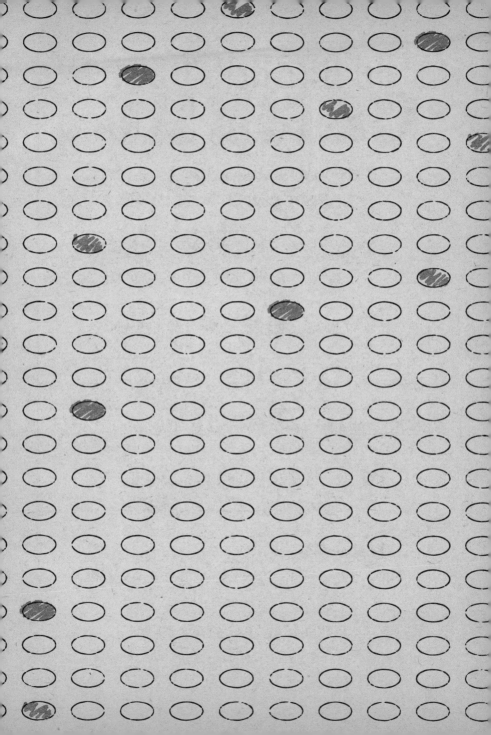

THE GREENE CODE OF CONDUCT

1) No matter how simple a job looks, always plan before you act.

2) Stay cool under pressure. A rattled crew is a mistake-prone crew.

3) Never con for love. Or even like.

4) Never rat. No matter what.

5) Focus today. Gloat tomorrow.

6) Know when to walk away. It's better to live and fight another day.

7) Never resort to violence, threats, or blackmail. They're messy and unreliable.

8) Never con for pure revenge. . . . But it's okay to get it along the way.

9) Only share the plans of a job with your crew. Loose lips sink ships.

10) Never con anyone who doesn't deserve to be conned. Never hurt innocent bystanders.

11) Don't use a battering ram when a crowbar will do.

12) Do your homework. Secondhand research yields D-minus results.

13) Practice, practice, practice. Then practice again.

14) Make sure it's worth it.

15) If you're going to pull a con, know how to pull a con in style.

THE GREAT GREENE HEIST CONS

KOBAYASHI MARU (THE RIGGING OF THE NOT-A-SCANTRON MACHINE): First seen in *Star Trek II: The Wrath of Khan*, the Kobayashi Maru is an exam administered to all command-track Starfleet cadets. Designed as a "no-win" scenario, the test is meant to gauge a cadet's character and command capabilities. Cadet James T. Kirk beats the test by reprogramming the simulator, and is awarded a commendation for "original thinking."

CARRIE NATION (CARMEN CLEAVER): Carrie Nation was a radical leader of the temperance movement, the crusade to reduce or prohibit the consumption of alcohol in the late 1800s and early 1900s. Nation described herself as "a bulldog running along at the feet of Jesus, barking at what he doesn't like," and was notorious for using a hatchet to destroy saloon and bar property.

ANAKIN SKYWALKER (VICTOR CHO): Jedi Knight Anakin Skywalker betrays the Jedi Order to save his wife from a prophesized death, though his betrayal actually leads to her passing. Skywalker embraces the dark side of the Force and becomes the Sith Lord Darth Vader, enemy of the Galactic Republic.

WINDOWS VISTA (THE NEW NOT-A-SCANTRON MACHINE): Windows Vista is a computer operating system designed by Microsoft. Released in 2006, Vista was criticized for security and performance flaws. Many users downgraded to the previous operating system, Windows XP.

DENNIS ECKERSLEY (MEGAN FELDMAN): A closer is a relief pitcher that specializes in getting the final outs of a baseball game, usually when the team is leading. Dennis Eckersley became a dominant closer in the latter half of his twenty-four-year Major League Baseball career. Credited with almost four hundred saves (preserving the lead at the end of a game), Eckersley was named to the Baseball Hall of Fame in 2004.

WHITE RABBIT (MEGAN FELDMAN LEADING LINCOLN MILLER AWAY FROM THE COPY ROOM): In *Alice's Adventures in Wonderland*, the White Rabbit leads Alice down the rabbit hole into Wonderland.

DENVER BOOT (THE SWITCHED LOCK THAT HOLDS KEITH IN PLACE): The Denver Boot is a wheel clamp used to prevent a car from being moved. They were given the nickname when the city of Denver began using them in the enforcement of parking tickets.

FALLOUT SHELTER (THE COPY ROOM CLOSET): Designed mainly during the Cold War (1950s to 1991), fallout shelters were constructed to protect people from radiation resulting from a nuclear bomb.

ROBOT IN DISGUISE (GABY'S BOUQUET): The bouquet was named in honor of the 1980s Saturday morning cartoon and toy line (and subsequent movies) Transformers, which are humanoid-shaped robots that "transform" into everyday vehicles. The cartoon theme song features the line, "Robots in disguise."

ACKNOWLEDGMENTS

It takes a really large crew to pull off a caper novel.

I am forever grateful for the guiding hand of my editor, Cheryl Klein, and the support and unwavering faith of my agent and friend, Sara Crowe. Thank you both for believing in me and Jackson Greene.

I also owe a huge debt of gratitude to all my draft readers: Brian Yansky, April Lurie, Francis Yansky, Sean Petrie, Jess Leader, Ginger Johnson, Annemarie O'Brien, Sue LeNeve, Larissa Theule, Mary Winn Heider, Stephen Bramucci, Marianna Baer, Linden McNeilly, and Katie Bayerl. I'd like to thank Jeff Miller from Pop a Lock for technical guidance and Veronica Medina Addison for suggestions on grammatical content.

A special thanks goes to Rachel Wilson, as her thoughts on omniscient POV opened the door for me to finish my first draft, and to Tim Wynne-Jones, for keeping me honest when the novel wasn't working. I would also like to acknowledge the Vermont College of Fine Arts and the Austin, Texas, writing communities for their continued support and cheers.

I am indebted to the entire Arthur A. Levine Books/Scholastic team: Arthur Levine, Emily Clement, Elizabeth Starr Baer, and Nina Goffi. You all don't get nearly enough credit for the work you do.

And to Crystal, Savannah, and the rest of my family, thank you for being patient and for letting me keep this little book a secret for so long. I promise it was worth the wait.

TO CATCH A CHEAT

"Mr. Greene," Dr. Kelsey boomed. "Mind stepping into my office? We have a lot to discuss."

Jackson followed the principal into his office, then covered his nose as he was overcome with a smell reminiscent of his Grandma Eunice's chitlins. "Dr. Kelsey, I think there's a dead animal somewhere in here."

"Don't be cute, Mr. Greene." Dr. Kelsey settled behind his desk and nodded toward a pair of brown loafers in the corner. "I ruined those running into the boys' locker room to shut off the water. By that point, the toilets had already flooded the gym." He steepled his fingers. "Tell me, where were you on Saturday afternoon?"

Jackson sat down across from Dr. Kelsey. "Saturday? Mr. James said the prank happened on Sunday."

"Mr. James should focus on security, not plumbing," Dr. Kelsey replied. "No, given the amount of damage, we suspect that the toilets were clogged on Saturday evening, after the boys' basketball practice. The faucets were turned on as well. So I'll ask again—where were you on Saturday afternoon, between five and eight o'clock?"

"At the library. Studying." Jackson focused on Dr. Kelsey's nose. He told himself not to blink, not to hesitate. "My dad dropped me off. I checked out books and everything."

"Did anyone else see you there?"

"I don't know. Maybe."

"Then you don't have an alibi."

"But I just said—"

"Let's be honest. A boy with your particular talents wouldn't have any problem sneaking out of a public library unnoticed." Dr. Kelsey pulled a black book bag from his bottom file cabinet. "We found this wedged behind a door. Almost like someone dropped it and forgot it."

"Or maybe someone left it there after school on Friday by mistake."

"Perhaps," Dr. Kelsey said. "Do you recognize it?"

"I think I saw it at Target," Jackson said. "Or maybe Walmart. On clearance. You know I'm a sucker for sales."

"Mr. Greene, I've been very lenient with you over the last few months. I would hate to go back to our weekly meetings and random locker searches."

Jackson glanced at the book bag again. The flap was decorated with stickers from *Rights of Warfare: Southern Seas*. "Just because it looks like Charlie's backpack doesn't mean it's his."

"Wait. It gets better." Dr. Kelsey pulled a small notebook from the bag. The letters JG were stenciled into the notebook's red leather cover. "Recognize this?"

"I've never seen that notebook before."

Dr. Kelsey flipped it open. "Are you sure? It looks a lot like your handwriting."

Jackson squinted at the notebook. He didn't want to admit it, but Kelsey was right. The writing even matched his standard coding system—but none of the messages made sense. "Anyone could have copied my handwriting."

"Admit it. You got sloppy. You got caught."

"But I didn't do it."

"Last chance, Mr. Greene," Dr. Kelsey said. "You were fortunate enough to avoid getting caught during the fiasco with the student council election a few months ago, but your luck will eventually run out. Believe me, it's better if you confess now. You'd only be looking at a five-day suspension." He returned the notebook and bag to the drawer. "I won't be so forgiving later."

Jackson chewed on his lip. The principal was bluffing. He *had* to be. "What about the new security system?" he finally asked. "Check the NVR."

Dr. Kelsey pounced. "And how do you know the security system uses a Network Video Recorder?"

Jackson rolled his eyes. "Dr. Kelsey, *all* modern security-systems use NVRs." He had actually heard about Kelsey's super high-tech NVR and sixteen-camera surveillance system from a number of people—Mr. James, the security guard; Megan Feldman, science geek/part-time con artist/seventh-period office helper/ex-cheerleader; and even Lincoln Miller, the Student Honor Board Chairman. But as tempting as it seemed, outside of taking note of the camera locations, Jackson didn't bother to learn much else about the system. He figured he had no need—he really *was* trying to stay retired.

"I bet you could even stream video from the NVR to your computer," Jackson continued. "Go ahead. Pull it up. That'll prove I didn't pull the prank."

"I can't. Someone stole the hard drive from the NVR," Dr. Kelsey said. "I'm sure you're going to say that you didn't have anything to do with that, either."

"Of course not," Jackson said. "But I'm betting you've already checked my locker to be sure."

"You're still on probation, Mr. Greene. I can check your person or belongings whenever I wish."

Jackson took a deep breath. "Isn't there some type of back-up?" he asked. "Like, maybe the cameras somehow—"

"Save the effort," Dr. Kelsey said. "I know you snuck in on Saturday because the cameras can only hold twenty-four hours of video before recording over the previous day's tape. Any trace of your break-in would be gone by Monday morning."

Jackson was tempted to pull out his notebook, just so he could capture all the facts. "Dr. Kelsey, I promise—I had nothing to do with this prank."

Dr. Kelsey grinned. No, he *smirked*. "That's fine. You don't have to talk. I'm sure I can eventually convince Charlie de la Cruz to speak up. Or maybe I'll chat with Hashemi Larijani. Or Charlie's new best friend, Bradley Boardman. It's funny how students start talking once you take away some of their perks."

"They don't have anything to do with this, Dr. Kelsey."

"And you do?"

Jackson loosened his tie. This was pointless. As far as Dr. Kelsey was concerned, he was guilty. He was sure the principal would march him in front of the Honor Board today if he could. And Jackson couldn't tell him what he'd actually been doing Saturday night—not without getting Gaby in trouble too.

It was time to bring in the big guns.

"Can I use the phone?" Jackson asked, already sliding forward in his chair. "I need to call my dad."